GARY KRIST'S

The Garden State

"What makes the book memorable is [Krist's] Updike-like incisiveness. He reminds us of how much fun reading can be."
—*The New York Times*

"A wonderful collection…smart, funny and affectionate. [Krist] likes his characters and he convinces us to like them, too."
—*Cleveland Plain Dealer*

"The nuances of family life are amusingly, affectingly probed by Krist…and finely honed with humor."
—*Booklist*

"Through these piquant human comedies, Krist takes us into family constellations that change with growing up, becoming old or getting divorced. Krist knows his territory and his people, pinning down their reality in a cultural ambiance that nourishes smiles of recognition."
—*Publishers Weekly*

The Garden State

SHORT STORIES BY

Gary Krist

VINTAGE CONTEMPORARIES
Vintage Books
A Division of Random House, Inc.
New York

FIRST VINTAGE CONTEMPORARIES EDITION, NOVEMBER 1989

Copyright © 1987, 1988 by Gary Krist

Library of Congress Cataloging-in-Publication Data
Krist, Gary.
    The Garden State: short stories / by Gary Krist.—1st Vintage contemporaries ed.
      p.   cm.—(Vintage contemporaries)
ISBN 0-679-72515-6 (pbk.): $7.95
I. Title.
[PS3561.R565G3   1989]
813'.54—dc20   89-40120
                                           CIP

Manufactured in the United States of America
10 9 8 7 6 5 4 3 2 1

This book is for my family,
a tribe of northern New Jersey,

and for Yen-Tsen,
without whom nothing.

Acknowledgments

For their encouragement and advice, I would like to thank Robert Wright as well as the members of my triweekly writing group. I would also like to thank The Millay Colony for the Arts for support during the writing of a portion of this book.

"Health" and "Ty and Janet" first appeared, in slightly different form, in *The Hudson Review*.

Contents

_____

The
Garden
State

Tribes of Northern
New Jersey

One of the first things I ever heard about my mother's husband was that he once tried to tip his dentist. He's from Czechoslovakia—Stiva Grencek is his real name—so he's not really wise to American ways. Just before he left Bratislava, the story goes, somebody told him that you were supposed to tip everybody in America, it was the custom. Stiva took the lesson to heart: Three weeks after he got to New Jersey, he went to the dentist to get his first American filling. The procedure went off without a hitch—he didn't feel a bit of pain—so, when the dentist told him to rinse, just as the chair back was coming up with its electric hum, Stiva tried to slip the guy a dollar bill. The dentist just stared at him. "Is not enough?" my mother's husband asked.

This story came by way of my father, so I guess I should've taken it with a grain of salt. When you're in ninth grade, though, you still believe a lot of what your father tells you (at least I did, but I've always been a late bloomer). And to tell the truth, it does sound like Stiva. Sure, nowadays he's more savvy—ever since he changed his name to Steve Green and married my mother—but he's still like that in some ways. Awkward. Not really at home. Or, to hear my father tell it, dumb.

We didn't approve of the match, my father and me. I guess
we thought that Mom could've done better. Not that we ever
said anything to her—God forbid we should tell her what to
do—but we like to think of Mom as kind of a class act, a
sophisticated-lady type, while Stiva, well, if there are any peasants
left in Czechoslovakia, Stiva must've been one of them. He's
thick—muscular, I guess—but on the short side, with thinning
blond hair and no eyebrows to speak of. My mother is tall and
elegant. She has long, wavy hair, tan-colored, with blond high-
lights she has done every six weeks or so. She wears Serengeti
sunglasses and oversized silver jewelry and dark-colored stock-
ings. My father always says that she sells so many houses because she makes any house she shows look more cosmopolitan.
"She *wears* a house, the way other women wear necklaces," is
how he puts it.

Ever since their divorce, my father has lived three blocks away
from my mother in Teaneck. That seems strange to some people,
but it really makes a lot of sense. My parents parted on very
good terms, even though my mother more or less forced the
separation (she decided that my father was a "confirmed old
bachelor" after all). So, when my mother's agency got this great
listing right in the neighborhood, she couldn't bear to sell it to
anyone she didn't know. She sold it to my father. And it worked
out fine at first: I could have dinner with my mother in one of
my houses and then have dessert with my father in the other.
And we were all close enough together to keep an eye on each
other.

Then Stiva came along. He's a mechanic out at the Exxon
station on Route 46. My mother met him two years ago, when
her Honda broke down on the way to a showing in Fort Lee.

2

Mom told us later that Stiva fixed her transmission with the technique of a true artist. And she loved his accent. So they started dating. Six months later, they were engaged.

The wedding was really the first time my father and Stiva spent more than a few minutes in each other's company. It was in June, and the reception was held in the backyard of the old house—cold cuts, green salad, and six cases of Spanish champagne spread out on tables under the tilting Italian poplars. It was a sunny, cool day, with a strong breeze that kept blowing the ends of the crepe tablecloths up into the potato salad. Bees were everywhere, hovering over the turkey roll, drowning themselves in everyone's drinks. Three people—including the pastor who had done the ceremony—got stung and had to leave early. But my mother was determined to make the reception a success. She hopped from table to table, waving away the bees and telling jokes that no one seemed to find as funny as she did. They were all too nervous about the bees, I think.

She put my father right between me and my girlfriend, Mona, at the table near the tool shed, as far away from Stiva as she could get us. She felt bad about this, we could tell, but she was worried that my father might say something to Stiva if they were any closer. I was getting worried, too. By halfway through the reception, Dad had drunk lots of champagne and had started talking about my mother's "incomparable human qualities," which I knew was a danger signal. Mona and I tried to talk to him about the microwave-popcorn account his ad firm was working on, but he wasn't buying it. Then, just when we thought we had convinced him to take a short walk around the block with us, he stood up on wobbly legs and announced: "A toast!"

The backyard went silent, leaving only the sound of the bees

3

buzzing around the wedding cake. My mother turned to us from across the yard with a look of panic on her face.

"I would like to propose a toast to my lovely wife," my father began.

"Ex-wife, ex-wife," Mona muttered under her breath.

"To my lovely ex-wife," my father corrected himself. He picked up his plastic glass of champagne and raised it. "A woman of grace and style, of character and good taste, in some respects," he added. I saw Mona swallow hard. "To use a metaphor that all of us here will understand, she is a Rolls-Royce in the garage of life. That she must now share this garage with, shall we say, a cheap European import—"

Mona and I grabbed him from both sides and pulled him back down into the chair.

"To Evelyn and Stiva!" shouted a fast-thinking neighbor from another table. "Hear, hear!" someone else responded, and then everyone—except my father, whose arms we had pinned to his sides—drank to the health of the new couple.

Stiva has never really forgiven my father for that toast, and though they've declared an uneasy truce since then, the cease-fire is always collapsing. Meanwhile, I find myself hopelessly in the middle. I try to spend alternate nights at each house, but if I miss a night in either place, I have to suffer the consequences—my father will mope around and talk about how much better the food must be at my mother's, while Stiva looks at me with suspicious eyes, suspecting a father-son plot against him.

Then there's my mother. "We've got to do something about these boys," she said to Mona and me over dinner one night. She had taken us to the La Crepe in Paramus Park Mall for a strategy session after a telephone argument between my father and Stiva. Apparently, my father had called and asked to talk with Stiva's "better half." Stiva, not understanding my father's "innocent turn of phrase" (as my father put it), got upset and called him a "hoodlum." The conversation degenerated from there, until my mother managed to crawl behind the couch and disconnect the phone cord from the modular jack.

"Your father seems to be having trouble adjusting," my mother said as we sat over our *café au lait*s. "He spends too much time alone, I think. He needs a friend, someone his own age, in, I suppose, the same situation." She put down her cup, making her bracelets clatter against the saucer. "Any candidates spring to mind?"

I thought immediately of Mr. Kingston, the shop teacher at the junior high, and of Mr. Knoeflhorn, the pharmacist with the big biceps, but neither one seemed even remotely imaginable as my father's companion. In fact, I couldn't imagine *anybody* with my father, especially a male anybody. These things take time to get used to.

"I've got it!" Mona said suddenly.

My mother's face lit up. "Who?" she said, leaning forward with a look of conspiracy on her face.

"Ernest Barnes, my mother's first husband's brother." Mona took a handful of her long, raisin-colored hair and flicked it back over her shoulder. "You've never met him, but he's very nice. He's a radio announcer, lives up in Dumont."

I looked at Mona, feeling somehow annoyed with her. She must have sensed it, because I felt her hand on my knee under the table then, squeezing my knee in reassurance. "Never been married," she added.

My mother's eyebrow went up. "How old?" she asked.

"Mid-fifties. A little fat, I guess. But a really normal guy. He'd be perfect."

My mother sat back and clapped her hands together once. "Wonderful," she said. "Josh, I count on you to get your father used to the idea. Think you can make that work?"

I nodded, resigned to the fact that what we were doing probably was for my father's own good. He did need somebody, somebody who'd been through whatever had to be gone through.

"And, Mona," my mother went on, "you can take care of things with Ernest?"

Mona smiled. "He likes to be called Ern," she said. "I'll wait for word from Josh, and then we can set up a date."

"Then it's settled," my mother said, dabbing her lips gently with her napkin. "Now, as for Stiva—Josh, I need your help on this, too. I thought it might be a good idea for you to ask Stiva to teach you how to fix cars."

"Cars," I groaned. I hated cars. Every car I had ever driven seemed to me to have a mind of its own. I was such a bad driver, in fact, that Mona refused to ride with me unless she was driving. "Does it have to be cars?" I asked.

"Oh, come on, Josh," my mother said. "It's something that Stiva is passionate about. He'd be honored if you asked him."

I looked up from my coffee and saw that my mother and Mona were both staring at me with the same pleading expression on their faces. I sighed. "There's a sale on overalls at The Gap next door," I said.

"They're on me," my mother said, obviously pleased. Then she took my hand in one of hers and Mona's in the other. "I know if we work together on this we can succeed," she said, and I got a sudden, delicious whiff of her lilac perfume. "I want us all to be happy," she said, bringing our hands together over the table. "Happy as a family of larks."

My father and I were playing Scrabble in the living room. It was a Wednesday night, mid-July, and it was hot—one of those hot, damp nights when people's car alarms seem to go off for no reason in the world. We were sitting with all of the windows open, and we could hear the sound of traffic from Route 4, which ran just beyond a fence in our backyard. The house stood at a slight bend in the highway, right at the foot of a long, gradual incline, so we always heard the giant trucks shifting to a lower gear as they started the long climb toward Hackensack, Fair Lawn, and those mysterious high places to the west of Pompton Lakes.

"Would you accept 'unaerobic'?" my father asked me after a long pause. He had been complaining all game of having too many vowels. "It means 'not promoting increased respiration,' as in 'weight lifting, an unaerobic exercise.' "

I arched my right eyebrow the way Mona always did to express skepticism. "Would it be in the dictionary?" I asked.

My father scoffed and then began snapping the tiles onto the board one by one around the word "rob." "Challenge me and we'll look it up," he said gleefully.

I decided against it. My father collected dictionaries—specialized ones on every topic from geology to horse-training—and he usually was able to find even his weirdest inventions in one or another of them. " 'Unaerobic' it is," I said finally and then tallied up his score.

"You seem quiet tonight, sport," my father said as he picked through the remaining tiles. "Didn't have a fight with Mona, did you?"

I looked down at my own rack of tiles. With three "R"'s, three "I"'s, and a "Q" in my hand, I decided it was as good a moment as any to ask him about Ern Barnes. "Hey, Dad," I began, keeping my eyes on my tiles, "Mona knows this guy, a news guy on the radio, her mother knows him, really, almost a relative, and he's kind of, I don't know, in the same boat as you—in his fifties, living in a house . . ."

"Living in a house," my father repeated.

"Yeah, you know," I went on, feeling the heat in my ears. "We thought you guys might have a lot in common, I guess."

"Since we both live in a house," my father said. He was teasing me, but I could tell that what I was saying had knocked him off-balance. He picked up his glass of ice water, wiped away the wet ring under it with his hand, and then put the glass down again. "Your mother put you up to this, didn't she," he said.

"Well," I began. The lights dimmed once as the refrigerator kicked into operation. "Yeah, she did."

My father took off the horn-rimmed glasses he wore only for Scrabble or reading. He placed them on the table in front of him. "You know, I've been thinking along these lines myself," he said; then he looked at me and held up his hands. "Let me know if any of this upsets you to talk about."

I shook my head.

"I mean, I'm not talking about romance here, and I hope your mother's not, either, because, I mean, I'm just not. But a friend, somebody who knows what it's like—living in a house, as you put it. We could talk." He picked up his glasses again and started opening and closing them. "Your mother thinks this'll get me off Stiva's back, I bet. What an operator that woman is, God bless her."

I cleared my throat. "His name is Ern Barnes," I said.

"Sounds normal enough. He's on the radio, you say? What do we want, a barbecue or something? Out in the backyard?"

He was going for it. I couldn't believe he was going for it. "A barbecue sounds good," I said. "Mona says he likes chicken."

"A man of good taste, obviously." My father put his glasses back on and started rearranging the tiles on his rack. "I'll call Mona about details," he said. Then, without looking at me, he added: "We'll start your three minutes from now, if you like."

"I like," I said, and tried to concentrate on my letters. But suddenly I felt this strange wave rolling over me. I had just helped to fix my father up with a date. I guess you would call it a date. What other word was there? "Iris," I said finally, desperate to be done with my turn. I put my "IRI" down on the board and counted up my meager score.

"Iris," my father mumbled, tipping the top of his glasses forward so that he could see the word better. "Hmm, anyone with an 'OS' could make 'Osiris' out of that, couldn't they."

"Proper noun," I said.

"But undeniably a classy word, no?"

My eyebrow went up again. One of our house rules was that any technically illegal word was allowable if it was classy enough and if you promised that you could've scored as many or more points with a legal, less classy word. It was one of my father's innovations, a variation to spice up what he said was an otherwise boring game. I looked at him and said, "Be my guest."

"Ha!" he cried, throwing down his two letters. "You have a good heart, son, I've always said that." He chose two more letters as I tallied up his score. Then he leaned back in his chair and shook his head. "It's your mother's heart you've got," he said, looking at me and smiling wistfully. Tiny points of sweat were beading up on his nose in the heat. "Yes, indeed," he whispered. Then: "Evelyn," he said.

"Cah-bu-re-tor," Stiva pronounced, pointing at a filthy hunk of metal with a Bic pen. "In-take Man-i-fold."

It was a sunny Saturday morning, and the two of us were stooped under the hood of my mother's Honda in the driveway of the old house. I was wearing the stiff new overalls my mother had bought for me. Stiva was in his blue mechanic's outfit from work—baggy, covered with grease smears, with the name "Steve" stitched in orange thread above the left-hand pocket. It was our first lesson in car repair.

"Wah-ter Pump," he went on, pointing to another part of the engine. I nodded vaguely. I was trying to remember everything he told me—it really was interesting, with all those wires and tubes and things—but I was also worried about my shirt, the sleeve of which had ripped on something while I was trying to change the oil. It was one of my favorite shirts.

"And this is what?" Stiva asked quickly, pointing at something he had named just a minute ago. It looked like a mechanical version of the hydras we used to study under the microscopes in biology class.

"Alternator?" I guessed.

Stiva's eyebrows fell. "Dis-tri-byoo-tor," he corrected me. Then he smiled. "Is very tough at first, I know." Punching me lightly in the shoulder, he said, "Old Steve shows you how to fix, no problem. Three weeks, we go to business together, you know so much."

I nodded and smiled, not sure if I had just agreed to go to the Exxon station with him in three weeks or if he had been suggesting as a joke that we start up a garage of our own. "Sure," I said.

"Is great, no? The way everything works in here? Very logical." The night before, when I had asked him to teach me about engines, Stiva had been so overjoyed that he'd hugged me. "Hey, Evelyn," he had shouted to my mother in the kitchen. "Josh wants seminar in car repair. From me!" "That's wonderful, dear," my mother had answered, coming out to us into the living room. "You bet, is wonderful," he had said. Then he took my mother in his arms and kissed her—a long, unexpectedly serious kiss. "Stiva, honey," my mother said. She was pushing him away, but she was smiling. "Behave."

Anyway, there *was* something wonderful about it, I guess. I had hardly ever looked under a car hood before, so everything was new to me, and more interesting than I'd imagined. Stiva explained to me how the gas came in, got mixed with air, then went to the cylinders, ignited, and drove the pistons. And to see him working on an engine was amazing. He had short, knobby fingers, but he managed somehow to maneuver them into tiny spaces to adjust a spark plug or check a fuel line. He could take off the wing nut on the air cleaner by twirling it with his thumb. I could see why my mother had been impressed.

"Then this is the alternator," I said, pointing to another part of the engine.

"Is right!" Stiva almost shouted. "You pick up very fast." Then he winked at me. "Pretty soon you can fix Father's car.

Save big bucks on repair, since he won't come to me to fix for free. Thinks maybe old Steve will unconnect his brakes, huh?" He winked and punched me again on the shoulder. "He don't trust his wife's new husband." Then, looking suddenly philosophical, he added: "Is too true, I think."

"No, no," I insisted weakly.

"I understand," he said, shaking his head sadly. "I have trouble with this, too. Is very strange here. Back home the first and second husband never meet, and here they must make friends."

I shrugged and stared hard at the alternator. "It just takes some getting used to," I said.

Stiva laughed. He picked up a rag and began wiping his hands with it. "Is not so easy getting used to," he said. "But tell Father that I try, try very hard. He should try, too, tell him."

"I'll tell him."

"Hey," he said then, picking up an oil can and holding it out to me. "You try, too, huh? Get used to old Steve."

I took the oil can from his hand. "I try, too," I said.

My father and I were at the windows of the upstairs front bedroom when Ern Barnes pulled up in front of the house. Mona had banished us from the backyard—our questions, she said, were making her so nervous that she couldn't get the charcoal lit—so we had stationed ourselves upstairs to get a quick look at Ern before we met him. We were both nervous. Neither one of us knew what to expect.

Ern climbed slowly out of the front seat of his battered Dodge Dart. He was a heavy man, balding, with a thick reddish beard that seemed to jut forward from his chin. He had a pipe in his mouth, and under his arm was a little white Chihuahua with a green T-shirt. Ern was wearing a light-blue shirt open at the collar, blue plaid shorts, black stretch socks, and white shoes.

"Jesus, he looks like somebody whose friends would call him 'Cap'n' or something," my father said.

"Dad," I warned him. Actually, I was relieved by Ern's looks. He could've been any number of my friends' fathers in their lawn-watering clothes.

"Mona didn't tell us about the Chihuahua," my father said.

Just then Ern looked up and saw us at the windows. He waved. "Damn," my father muttered, waving back. "How embarrassing. Come on."

We ran downstairs and opened the front door to find Ern wiping his white shoes on the mat. The Chihuahua under his arm turned to us and said, "Yip!"

"You must be Ern Barnes," my father said, holding out his hand. "I'm Wallace Lurie, and this is my son, Josh."

"Pleased to meet you, Wallace, Josh," he said and shook our hands. His voice was deep and smooth and melodious, even with the pipe between his teeth. "And this is Dan," he went on, shifting the Chihuahua under his arm.

"Yip!" said Dan again.

"Dan has a tendency to get obnoxious once in a while," Ern said apologetically, "but he should be all right until about nine o'clock, which is when he usually goes to bed. Mind if he joins us till then?"

"Not at all, not at all," my father said, with a generous tone I found encouraging. "Just bring him on through to the back. Mona's out there getting the hibachi started."

We walked single-file through the hallway and kitchen—Ern looking around appreciatively and making polite comments

13

about the decor—and then through the back door into the yard. We found Mona bending over the hibachi, blowing puffs of air over the coals. She straightened up and smiled, then frowned when she saw Ern.

"Uncle Ern," she said, with disappointment in her voice, "you wore those awful shorts after all."

"Now, Mo-Mo," he said, and kissed her on the forehead. He turned to us: "Mona called me up last night to discuss my outfit for today. She has this notion that my taste in leisure wear leaves something to be desired."

"That's putting it mildly," Mona said blandly.

"What do kids know, Wallace, am I right?"

"Ha-ha," my father blurted, maybe a little too heartily.

"I see you've dressed The Terror, too," Mona said, taking Dan from under Ern's arm. "Hey, sweet." She scratched him behind the ears, making Dan yip a few more times and start licking her on the chin. "OK," she said then, taking charge, "the chicken will be at least an hour. So who wants a drink?"

For the next few hours, the four of us sat in lawn chairs around the picnic table, making conversation. Ern and Mona did most of the talking at first, mostly about Mona's mother, Joan. Ern still visited her, even though it was twenty years since she and his brother had divorced. "Joan is like a sister to me," Ern told us, "which makes Mona my niece, in spirit if not by blood. Why don't we have a word for that in English—your brother's ex-wife's daughter by her other husband? After all, I held her in my arms the day after she was born. She even spit up on me, for heaven's sake."

"I know the feeling," I said. "She did the same thing on me the night of the junior prom." Mona frowned, dipped her finger in her drink, and flicked me with a drop of gin-and-tonic.

"And did she do it as charmingly seventeen years later?" Ern asked.

I smiled and glanced at Mona. Ern was great, I wanted my glance to tell her. He was just the kind of friend my father needed. Just the kind of decent, at-ease person who could help him out. I tried to imagine my father and Ern becoming friends, doing whatever middle-aged male friends do—getting up at six to go fishing, filling out tax returns. It was almost conceivable.

The only hitch, of course, was my father himself. Somehow, he didn't seem to be responding to Ern in the same way I was. Instead of getting more relaxed as the evening wore on, he seemed to be getting more nervous. He laughed too loudly at everything, told weird, irrelevant anecdotes, and kept on getting up to check the hibachi. The only one who seemed more nervous than my father, in fact, was Dan, who kept running back and forth under the picnic table, his nails making a sound against the slate like someone shaking a pair of dice.

Things only got worse after we ate. Mona and I had agreed beforehand to excuse ourselves after the cheesecake—there was a sale at Stern's, we would say, that couldn't be missed—but every time we even hinted at leaving, my father would furiously kick my sneaker under the table and give me a look of sheer panic. Mona, however, was firm. "C'mon, Josh," she'd say meaningfully, "my mother really needs those sheets and pillow-cases." (flurry of kicks under the table) "Just another minute," I'd insist. "I want to hear the end of this story." (withering glance from Mona) "But that *was* the end of the story," Ern would say. (more kicks) "I must've missed something, then. What did the guy do after the bomb squad showed up in the broadcast booth?" (pointed sigh from Mona) "Yes"—this from my father—"I think I missed that part, too."

15

It was at one of these moments, just when we reached a point of balance between Mona's impatience and my father's hysteria, that Ern started talking about his group. "I guess there are about a dozen of us guys," he explained as the sun dipped behind the maples that shielded us from the exhaust fumes of Route 4. "We get together every month or so, just to talk about things, issues, what it's like being gay and middle-aged, et cetera. Sometimes we play golf, too." Ern took a sip of his drink and then looked right at my father. "It's helped a lot of us make our transition, Wallace. And it's enjoyable. We take field trips sometimes. To a Broadway show in the city. Or else we'll have a picnic at the Oradell Reservoir."

"A picnic," my father repeated.

"In fact," Ern went on, stretching the knuckles of his hands, "we're having a meeting on Thursday. It's at my place, in Dumont. Maybe you'd like to stop by, Wallace. To meet some of the other guys." Ern paused. In the silence we could hear the distant whine of a tractor-trailer. "Wallace?" he asked finally.

My father cleared his throat. "Ern, kids," he began, looking down at his hands in a way that told me we had trouble. "I think this is a great thing that we're all trying here. A really great thing." He stopped and scratched his shoulder in concentration. "But I have to tell you that I just can't go through with it. I sit here and listen to what you're telling me—field trips, open discussions—and I think, Yes, this is the way I should be going, but somehow it's not me. I'm not ready for this, I guess." He got up from the table, sending Dan clicking to the other side of the patio. "Look, if it's not too rude of me, I'll be leaving now to go bowl a few games at the Eclipse Bowl. It helps me think, bowling. Forgive me."

Ern was looking over at the glowing coals in the hibachi. "And you'd like us to be gone when you get back?" he asked in that smooth, deep voice.

My father paused a second before answering. "Ern," he said finally, "I think I would."

My father stood behind his chair for another second. He took a deep breath and then made a sudden, vague gesture with his hands. "I'm a family man," he said quietly. Then he turned and walked away from us into the darkened house, making the screen door screech as he slid it shut behind him.

Weeks passed. The temperature climbed. In every backyard, high in the branches of the tallest trees, cicadas grated through the long afternoon. Overhead, tiny silver planes flashed as they caught the sunlight on their descent to Newark Airport. There was only a flat, vinyl-tasting breeze to cool things off. And on every lawn in Teaneck, sprinklers swept back and forth, spattering the sidewalks, creating small, warm rivulets that carried cut grass and candy wrappers along the gutters of the street.

My mother and I were sliding around the backyard of the old house on our knees, pulling dandelions. She was wearing a damp, flowered kerchief on her head, and her hands were stained grass-green. It was August in northern New Jersey, when most mothers and children had already headed down the shore in station wagons stuffed with plastic shovels, boxes of elbow macaroni, and polyurethane rafts. Mostly it was fathers who stayed behind in the neighborhoods these days. This, at least, had not changed in Teaneck—the fathers stayed behind in August. To work. To watch over. To care for the sacred lawn.

"So your father finally let Ern visit again?" my mother asked. She threw another uprooted dandelion into the plastic pail I held for her.

"Finally," I said. "He came over for dinner day before yesterday. They talked about the Yankees, though I don't think either one of them really cares about baseball."

My mother smiled. "I hope your father appreciates how patient Ern's been with him."

"I think he does," I said, though I wasn't so sure. After Ern had left that night, my father had said to me, "Ern's a little bit pushy, don't you think? A little bit preachy?"

"Well," my mother went on, "Ern or no Ern, your father's still on Stiva's case. Whenever he calls now and Stiva answers, he just hangs up without saying anything. It makes Stiva furious. You can practically see the little jets of steam coming out of his ears."

I laughed. I had seen Stiva in that kind of anger—one morning, before our weekly lesson, when he opened a new box of spark plugs and found that all of them were dead.

"Your father does it on purpose, I think," she said then, thoughtfully. A thin blade of grass was pasted onto her cheek with sweat. She looked beautiful, I thought. "Listen, Josh," she went on, "those terrible little wheels have been turning in my head again. I've been thinking of reviving the old end-of-summer barbecue tradition. We could set up the long table under the poplars like we used to."

I stared at her in disbelief. We hadn't had the end-of-summer barbecue since the divorce. "Are you kidding?" I said. "That was always Dad's thing. He'd never come with somebody else hosting it, especially Stiva."

"That's just it, Josh. Your father *will* be hosting it, or at least cohosting it. We'll all four of us share the duties."

She was facing me with that look of eternal hope in her eyes. "I don't know, Mom," I said after a few seconds.

"Oh, don't be such a skeptic, Josh. Aren't you willing to try, at least?"

I put down the pail. "Why do we have to push so hard? Some things work better if you just let them run their own course."

She scraped some dried mud off the side of her sneaker with the weeding tool. "You sound like your father now," she said.

A huge bumblebee appeared and started circling heavily around the pail. My mother and I watched it absentmindedly for a few seconds before it buzzed away and disappeared into the poplars. "Oh, damn," I said, more to myself than to my mother. It had been a long, exhausting summer for me. I hadn't been able to find a job, so I was left in the thick of things without anywhere to escape to. And somehow, no matter what I did, I felt like I was being disloyal to somebody. Agreeing to this picnic would be the same thing all over again, only I wasn't exactly sure who I'd be betraying by agreeing to it.

My mother put her hand on my sneaker. "This will help," she said. "Mona thinks so, too."

My jaw tightened. So Mona was in on this. She hadn't said a word to me. I looked up at my mother's sweaty kerchief. The last time I go along, I told myself, the very last time. "So this would be Labor Day?" I asked.

My mother threw a dandelion into the air in celebration. "I'm so glad, Josh," she said. "I figure we can tell everyone to come at one o'clock." She got up and brushed the grass from her knees. "We can have all three grills going at once, just like the old days."

I was still crouching on the grass, looking into the half-filled bucket. "School will be starting the day after," I said.

"Well, then, we can celebrate the start of your senior year, too." She stood above me with her hands on the hips of her prewashed jeans. It occurred to me, for the first time, that maybe I understood this whole situation better than she and Mona did.

"Now, let's hustle in and get some iced tea," my mother said then, sounding a lot like Beedy Fox, the football coach at the high school. "I'd say we've earned it."

The Lurie end-of-summer barbecue (now the Lurie/Grencek aka Green end-of-summer barbecue) had always been the big event of the Labor Day weekend in our neighborhood. Everyone on the block would get involved: Mrs. Warndial from next door would make her famous carrot-and-raisin salad, the D'Agostino twins would hang their volleyball net on the other side of the sticker-bushes, and old Mr. Murano, the widower with the cherry trees, would bring along his accordion to play Italian love songs as the sun went down.

It had been a neighborhood tragedy when my parents got divorced and the tradition ended. Labor Day became a gloomy time on our block. No one else even considered hosting their own end-of-summer barbecue. It would have been too strange, somehow. Almost sacrilegious.

That's why the return of the tradition this year was such good news to everyone, and why all of the guests arrived in an especially festive mood. People fell wholeheartedly into the old routines, as if they were parts of a holy ritual that had just been reinstated. Mrs. Goldblum and Olga Zervas even did their usual rumba around the stunted peach tree, saying that they hadn't danced together since the last Lurie barbecue.

Ern, who had been invited with my father's approval, had shown up—without Dan this time—at around two with a cherry cheesecake and two Danish rings for my mother. This was the first time the two of them had met, but they seemed to like each other instantly. My mother told him that she had started listening to him on the radio news every morning, and he seemed sincerely flattered by that. Then she took him by the arm and led him around the yard, introducing him to everyone as a local celebrity. He laughed every time she said it, and looked modest.

As jolly as anyone that afternoon, strange as it may seem, was my father. He stood over the three Smoky Joes at the edge of the yard, flipping hamburgers and Italian sausages, laughing at everyone's jokes. He had surprised me (again) by readily agreeing to my mother's plan when I told him about it. "I think it's a fine idea, Josh," he had said. "And don't look so gloomy. I won't poison Stiva's beer, I promise."

In fact, I had to admit to myself—as I sat under the poplars with Mona and the Puglieses from next door—that the two of them were behaving with amazing civility to each other. My father had served Stiva one of the first of the sausage sandwiches, heaped high with steaming peppers and onions. Stiva had taken a bite and announced, "You are the master, Wallace. Is perfect!" My mother had caught my eye then, from across the crowded yard. I lifted my beer to her, and she smiled.

It was going so well, in fact, that none of us—not even the supreme tactician herself—foresaw any danger when, toward the tail end of the afternoon, Stiva and his colleagues from the gas station started gathering around my mother's car in the driveway at the end of the yard. It was natural, after all, for a group of garage mechanics in a social setting to start talking shop under the hood of somebody's car. What we didn't think about was the fact that Stiva would inevitably want to show off the talents of his young student in car repair—his stepson, his prodigy.

"Hey, Josh!" Stiva yelled to me. He was standing in the middle of his group of friends in front of the car. The barbecue was almost over at this point—the sun had already sunk behind the roof of the Casillo house out back—and everyone was getting quieter, sitting back with their stomachs full of potato salad and Rolling Rock beer, enjoying the tapering off of a well-spent summer afternoon. "Come, Josh," Stiva shouted, "show these no-good guys how much I teach you."

I was standing with my father at the time, holding a garbage bag while he emptied the doused coals from the three Smoky Joes. He froze for a second. "How much he *teach* you?" my father said.

I tried to be nonchalant. "Oh yeah, Stiva's giving me car-repair lessons, didn't I tell you?"

"Hey, Joshy," Stiva persisted. "You help your father later. Is OK, Wallace?"

"Car-repair lessons," my father said simply.

"Hey," Stiva shouted. He was getting embarrassed in front of his friends. Everybody else in the backyard seemed to have stopped talking. My mother and Mona and Ern—all three of them—were gone, in the house washing glasses. I held open the garbage bag, unable to move.

My father turned with the Smoky Joe in his arms. "My son is busy with his father right now," he said across the yard. "And he certainly won't root around under car hoods at your command."

"Dad," I said under my breath, but I knew it was too late. Stiva was already puffing air from his cheeks. I could see the anger building in his body from twenty yards away.

Stiva took a slow breath. "Josh, you are coming, or no?"

"Don't move, Josh," my father said quickly. Then, to Stiva: "He's too busy to humor you now. He's got more important things to do."

Stiva said something in Czech and then kicked the side of the garage. "Is too much!" he shouted, pacing back and forth in front of his friends, who stood behind him with their hands in their pockets, trying to look interested in the car. "I try again and again with you, Wallace, and is just no good. So, now, get out! Is all I can say."

"Get out of my own backyard?" my father sneered.

"Is MY backyard now, buddy. MY wife, MY house, MY family. And I say out."

My father stared at him. The other guests were all silent now, watching in horror. "You want me out, I'm out," he said finally, and he threw the Smoky Joe halfway across the yard and into the garden plot, where it fell with a thick, dull thud. He stalked across the lawn toward the side of the house, muttering under his breath. Then he stopped. "Are you coming, Josh?"

I was still standing there with the garbage bag in my hands.

"I'm asking you to come with me, son," my father said slowly. Stiva was staring at me hard from the garage. The door to the kitchen was still closed. Everyone was looking at me.

I decided. My father smiled and put his arm around my shoulder as I joined him at the edge of the yard. "Good night, everyone," he shouted to the guests as we walked away. "Thanks for coming. Next year at my house." And then we were gone, without looking back, without saying a word to my mother.

It was already turning dark as we walked together down the sidewalk toward our house. My father's arm was still around my shoulder, and we walked slowly, looking up into the branches of the anemic sycamores that lined our street from end to end. Crickets were chirring in the bushes, stopping as we passed and then starting up again behind us.

"Well, Josh, I've done it again, I guess," he said finally.

"Uh-huh, you did."

"Damned if I know what gets into me. That man just gets to me, you know?" He looked over at me with a crooked sort of smile on his face. "You should've told me about the car lessons. I wouldn't have minded at all. I just wish you told me."

"Sorry," I said. Then: "He's really not such a bad guy, you know. You two might even like each other."

"Yeah, yeah, I know." He stopped and kicked a white piece of gravel back into a flower bed. "It's just that I still feel a little like your mother's husband, even after all this time. Sorry I put you on the spot that way. Guess I've got a real talent for that."

"I guess."

We reached our front yard. Together we stood at the end of the walk and looked over the house, as if we were appraisers or prospective buyers. The sound of traffic was loud from the highway. It almost sounded like a brook in the backyard—a tiny country stream.

"Poor Ern," my father said. "We left him all alone back there."

I shrugged and looked down at my father's shoes. "He'll be all right."

"Well, sport," my father said then, "next year at about this time you'll be going off to college." He pulled me closer and quietly chanted, "Go, State, rah rah." He chuckled softly and then paused a moment before adding: "It'll be good for you to get out of Teaneck. Give you a chance to worry about yourself for once."

I smiled, but it seemed to me, as we stood there in front of the dark house, that college was a long way off. There was the next week to get through, the next month. And I knew that before the year was up, my father would have to shift gears finally, like those trucks on the Route 4 hill, scraping their clutches at the start of the long climb to Passaic County.

My father was shaking his head. "Just one more year," he said. "Think we'll be ready?"

Ty and Janet

Animals

No animals, period. She was really strict on this. What about cats? I ask her. No, she says, cats are dirty. Dirty. I say, What do you think they're doing with the tongues all over, tasting themselves? That's saliva, she says, saliva's got germs, especially cat saliva. So, OK, no cats. Gerbils—she won't even talk. So, finally, she agrees on fish, tropical fish. Fine. I read up a little, get a few books from the library, go to the pet store. The guy there—he's got this yellowy glass eye, I remember this about him, and this smell kind of like stale tobacco—the guy sells me a twenty-gallon and says, Whattaya want, some nice guppies? I say, No, you're gonna go, you go right. So he shows me these little jobs, really nice colors, zinging around, and he says, These are neons. Fine, I say, let's have some neons. He shows me other things, too—angels, mollies (they're only black, he says, but they're cheap and they give the tank a classical look). In short, he gives me what he calls "a starter outfit"—filter, tank, fish, food, everything—$97.35 with the tax. I say to him, Jesus, this outfit runs I bet for half that in the city, Canal Street they sell this kind of stuff. He says, So go to Canal Street.

This is a Saturday, Janet's out bowling with her girlfriends, so I figure she'll be real surprised to come in and see this thing

I got set up—angels sailing across the tank, neons zinging around. It's the angels I love, though. Jesus, the way they sail across that tank? Slow, like little skinny kings.

Anyway, Janet comes home twelve-thirty, one o'clock. I'm sound asleep in the chair in front of the tank. First thing she says, she shakes me awake, middle of the night, and she says, I quote, "What's this business we got now?" I say, You agreed on fish. She says, Goldfish is one thing, I didn't expect Marine World. I say, Just look at those angels if you want to know why I went whole hog.

So, she can live with the aquarium is the upshot. I do feeding, cleaning the filter, everything, she takes a look in the tank once in a while. Anyway, pretty soon I start to spend some time with the fish. I get into this thing: I wake up two, three in the morning and put on a dimmer lamp in the living room and watch them sleep. Sleep is I guess what you call it. They get all quiet and motionless at night, down near the little plastic sand castle with the bubbles coming out of the moat. And they just stay there, moving a little fin now and then, and I watch them. One night even Janet comes out into the living room. Insomnia, she says. I say, Come over here and take a look at this. She sighs, but she comes over. I make room for her on the kitchen chair I brought in, and we sit there watching the fish. Dim orange light, the bubbles making a quiet sound, her smell like the rye bread from her work. Then she puts a hand on my shoulder and says, "What are they, Ty, resting?" Resting, she says. I like that. So I say, Yeah, they're resting. So we sit there, she's in her night-gown, hair out to here, and we watch the fish rest.

Shit, God knows what happens sometimes, though. You come home from the plant, you don't know what-all you'll find— fish corpses, shredded tailfins bouncing up and down on the jet stream. I come home one day I see this angel—my favorite angel—lying on the ground about five feet from the tank in a little puddle of water, dead. I say, "What've we got, suicide now?" This angel jumped out of the damn tank, just like that, boom, it's dead, no chance in hell of bringing that thing back to life. Dried up like an old wallet. And it's like: What did I do? Cheap food? Not enough "greenery" in the tank, or what?

It's like when DePaula up and quits on me on a Wednesday afternoon. What's the reason? Bad vibes, he says. What vibes, it's the buzz of the flywheels you're feeling, for Chrissake. He says, The other guys feel it, too, you ask them. Like shit, though. Three days later I see DePaula behind the five-dollar win-place-show at the Meadowlands, pulling down probably two times the money, from what you hear. A crock, I tell you. Win, place, fucking *show*, for Godsake.

I go to the zoo a lot—I'm kind of this animal lover?—and I was at the zoo this once, looking at the penguins behind the glass there. They're all bunched up at the door at the back of the habitat, they call it, jerking their heads—vip, vip—and I figure the guy who feeds them is out there. Sure enough, the door opens, and this young guy in a lumber jacket with a beard and galoshes walks in with this sky-blue bucket full of fish. So he's taking the fish out one at a time and sticks it down the gullet of one of the penguins. He does this for a few minutes, and pretty soon, with all the penguins and them all looking more or less alike, the guy I guess loses track of who's had his fish and who hasn't. So what he does is start just holding out the fish and moving it from one beak to another, until finally one of the penguins opens his beak and swallows it. This goes on, he sticks a fish in front of one, it turns away, he moves it to the next, this one just stares at it, dumb; same thing down the line until he gets to one that grabs it, tosses his head back, and, slurp, down it goes. After this, the guy comes out and I go up to him. He smells like antiseptic and fish, this guy. So: What's this routine you got with these birds, I ask him. And he tells me: he loses track of who's had the fish and who hasn't, so what he does, he gives each bird a chance at the next fish. Any penguin's got a fish in his gullet will have to think a minute before swallowing another; any penguin with no fish yet'll snap the thing up pronto. So they *tell* you, he says, the penguins *tell* you if they've got their fish. Well, I think about this for a few minutes and then it hits me: it's beautiful, this guy and his penguins. It strikes me, I can't even say. I leave the zoo, drive through the Bronx, I don't even want to see anything else.

Janet thinks I'm crazy on this. One night we're sitting in front of the TV, she's got this box of animal crackers on her lap—the homemade kind they make at her place?—and I watch her take a cookie out of the box, put it in her mouth, take another, do the same thing—all the while she's got her eyes glued on the TV. Finally, I gotta say something. "Baby, you don't know if you're eating a gorilla, an elephant, or what, you eat those things that way." She looks at me like I'm cracked or something. Then she says it. She sticks this jaguar or panther cracker in her mouth and says, mouth full: "What difference does it make? They all taste the same anyway."

Bread

I don't do much baking any more, not like the old days when everybody would line up with a loaf's worth and beat the day-lights out of it, little clouds of flour rising and everybody joking:

"No loafers here!" and "We've got enough flour here for the Rose Bowl Parade!"; to which my famous comment that once: "At yeast!" Nowadays I do mostly paperwork—payroll, supply ordering. The bakers don't usually like you to lend a hand (union rules), unless of course they're in a crunch. But every so often I'll want to make a loaf myself and they say fine and shove it in with theirs.

When I started I was part-time—still in school—worked from seven to eight-thirty and three to six. We were much smaller then. One baker—Angel, a Cuban, used to take the bus up from Union City at 4:00 A.M. every day. I used to imagine him alone on that dark bus, passing empty sidewalks and stores, his hands working at that grip-spring that was supposed to build up his forearms. You always knew where Angel was—he creaked.

Ty would show up after detention—around four, when everyone in charge was gone—and I'd feed him doughnuts, one after the other—crullers, rolls, muffins. Who knows where he put it all? He joked once that he did the old finger-down-the-throat routine after he left, which was disgusting (but funny, because I never believed him). He ate a dozen glazed bow ties once and looked yellow afterward. I had to smile at him, though, with his cowlick and that queasy look and that empty doughnut tray in front of him. I kissed the white glaze off his upper lip and gave him a half-dozen crullers to take home. You could get away with that back then; nowadays I'd be the one to notice the cash discrepancy and lecture everybody about not forgetting to write down their take-homes.

Ty used to pick me up afterward in his mother's electric-blue Toyota. He'd call me "Bread Pudding" and ask me to smuggle out some of our homemade animal crackers for him. He was a year out, working an evening shift at PSE&G, and I was still a junior when he finally asked me. Hell, I was still doing things like running for class treasurer ("Lesser Is More" was my campaign slogan). Of course I said yes, Sybil and my mother be damned.

We got married up in Bear Mountain in the middle of January. Eloped, really, though we did end up convincing at least our mothers to drive up together in Mom's Omni for the ceremony. Neither of them cried. Mom called Dad right after and yelled at him for not coming, even if he did think I was too young. Then she and Mrs. Steinbock gave us a few packages wrapped in aluminum foil and got in the car. They never made it home, though; not in the Omni, at least. They stalled on 9W and couldn't turn the engine over. Ty had to go down and jump-start them. I sat in bed in my new red satin nightgown, doing crosswords and laddergrams until Ty came back at 4:00 A.M.

Of course I quit school and started full-time at the bakery. A working couple. I'd bring home bags of rolls and bread and sometimes that's all we'd eat—bread and wine. We'd laugh, and Ty would turn on a lamp and say, "I made this electricity today; you like it?" and I'd start throwing pumpernickel rolls at him. The first month, we did dishes three times. The garbage would go out only when the piles of paper plates and pizza boxes started to tip over.

The whole thing (the marriage, I mean) never crashed, really. It just tinkled, gradually, like icicles falling off the eaves when the weather warms up. I kept waiting for things to happen that never did. Other things happened. I'd get depressed all of a sudden, and Ty would get mad at me because I couldn't tell him why. Then he'd get depressed, too. He hated his job, especially after the promotion. Some of the older guys who were his buddies wouldn't even speak to him after. God, that burned him. Once, about a year and a half after we got married, he came home and drank too much and started pushing me around, yelling at me. He's not that big a man, though; I shoved him back over his mother's hand-embroidered ottoman and he hit his head and was out, literally out, for about two minutes. That humbled him. Next day he said he wanted to have a talk about getting some pets.

So what happened to us? I don't know, it was like putting two chemicals together and waiting for a reaction that never comes. Both chemicals just turn blue (ha!). Sybil was right about Ty, what can I say? Looking back on it, I wonder how I ever said yes. And why it took me four years to realize my mistake. I think I have this problem: I stay in situations too long. Things may be bad, I always figure, but they could be a lot worse. When things start to press on me, I can always make myself a hot cup of soup, sit in my armchair, and do the jumble in the paper. Then I can start fresh. I can tell myself that I have what I want.

Except for the drinking, I could have made it with Ty. And it really was rare that he got mean drunk; he really is kind of a gentle man—a sad, gentle man. I'd come home and find my crossword books behind his armchair. He'd been at them, filling in all the blanks in the ones I'd started. Nonsense words like "plark" and "whisbox."

And there were other effects. I mean it shouldn't matter, I guess. But it did. And I just kept trying. I came home one night in one of my Let's-see-if-we-can't-revive-this-thing-again moods, and three minutes after I'm in the door I already see that it's a lost cause, that *he* is a lost cause. So I told him I had to go, did he understand why? He didn't, and so I left, really left—suitcase, checkbook, and all. I left him sitting on the toilet with a glass of dessert wine in his mitt. My Tyrone.

It wasn't until I was on the second set of stairs that the softball rose in my throat and almost made me turn around. . . .

Wine

I thought the guy was putting us on. But, I mean: the Tarrytown Country Club; we all paid through the nose. But "foxy," Jesus! There was even a couple of laughs when he said it. But then the next guy looks up and says, "Mahogany, violets, plums." I'm sitting there thinking, Oh Christ, but the guys, they're saying, "No, all that's in there if you taste, taste actively with the nose as well as the tongue." So I try, I take a sip, thinking Violets. Plums (I don't even begin to know what the mahogany taste is), but anyway, damned if I don't taste like a plummy taste? The violets, maybe the smell is kind of flowery, but I really can taste the plums. Other people, same thing. The lady next to me raises her hand and says, "Mint, too, right?" And the two guys look at each other and one says, "Well, eucalyptus anyway."

So this is how it started. Tuesday nights Janet's out with Sybil, so why not? My grandfather used to love the stuff. Lots of people dropped out (including the mint lady, I might add), but me, I stay two full rounds of classes, we do everything,. Rhone wine, Alsace-Lorraine, everything. At the end we have this big tasting party, and by midnight people are yelling out things like "Dead cat!" and "Pepto-Bismol!" and even the instructors laugh, they're crocked just like the rest of us.

The guys at the plant, they're always on to me about this, you know, kidding me about that Leatherette case I'd bring to work when I had a tasting that night, with the holes cut out in the Styrofoam for the bottle and glasses? We have this kind of jokey relationship I like to maintain in my area. Last Christmas they gave me this nice bottle of Beaujolais and a corkscrew made out of a piece of driftwood from Point Pleasant. It's part of our thing, the guys and me—the wine thing. It's, like, I'm their supervisor, but they can kid me on the wine thing. I find this appropriate, I think.

Anyway, with the course, I start to buy on my own. First I stick to the cheaper stuff—five, six bucks—but pretty soon I figure, What the hell, I'll spring for ten, twenty. It gives me pleasure, and we're doing OK, Janet's working, I'm working, the apartment's rent-control, so I buy the good stuff. Champagne I buy; some good Burgundies. I start to go into Sauternes. Now, this is an interesting wine, Sauternes—very sweet, a dessert wine, as it were. What they do, they let the grapes stay on the vine way late, this is only in a special area of Bordeaux, France, now, they let the grapes stay way late until this mold crops up, I kid you not. "Noble rot" is what they call this mold thing, and it starts shriveling up the grapes and concentrating the sugars, and then they pick the things one by one, and the wine is sweet, but not Mogen-David sweet: complex sweet. There's acid, too, in the grapes, and the acid and the sugar balance out, and it's incredible. An arm and a leg the stuff costs; I never told Janet what I paid, she'd raise one holy ruckus, that's for sure. One trouble is you've got to drink the whole bottle in one day or else the whole thing spoils on you and, bam, there's your twenty bucks down the drain literally, and I mean literally.

All right, so maybe it gets to be a regular thing, like. But the stuff tastes so good you don't want to stop at half the bottle even if you want to. Half-bottles they charge you highway robbery. "We've got *this* on top of everything now!" This from you-know-who. "On top of everything," like what's everything, you know? She doesn't do too bad herself with the Gilbey's, either. You're just a cheaper drunk than me, that's all the difference, blah, blah, blah, before you know it she's out the door again spending the night at Sybil's.

That time she left—she left for a month once—it was kind of like that. She comes home, I don't know, hot to trot, like she must've seen some hot new pastry boy at work, and I'm already halfway through a Château Coutet 1979, so who's in the mood, y'know? This she finds unacceptable. "There exists no way to get through to you," she says, putting on the Sybil voice, and pretty soon I hear her in the bedroom getting the big green suitcase out of the storage space over the closet. I decide to play it close, the thing'll blow over, maybe if I drink some water and think sexy thoughts I can take her from behind while she's stuffing leg warmers into the suitcase. But: no way. I'm in the bathroom when she's ready to leave, she stands in the doorway looking at me on the throne with a suitcase and a loaf of three-grain bread in her arms. I look up at her—ugly fluorescent lighting—and "You're not leaving," I tell her. Bam, she's out the door without a word.

She was gone for one month. At Sybil's, she said, but I don't know, Sybil'd never let me talk to her. *She* had to call me, this was the deal. I'd come home, I'd see evidence—another drawer emptied out, the blender gone, once she even fed the fish and

left a note: "Have you taken a look at that algae buildup?"—
as if she cared. The weird thing is, though, once she's gone, I
stop drinking, cold turkey. The bottles just sit there on the rack—
fifteen-, twenty-dollar bottles, they've got no temptation for me
any more. All the while, I know she's coming back, so I'm just
sort of waiting. I sit up with the fish, I read the newspaper. And
she does come back, one month later to the day. She gives me
a call: "Things work out; things don't work out. Put a fire on
in the fireplace." So I do, I put on one of those supermarket-
log jobbies and, can you believe it, I break open this special
bottle of Perrier-Jouet champagne, with the painted flowers
hand-painted on the bottle, 1978? It's, like, it just doesn't occur
to me that this might be a problem, I'm so out of the habit.
Anyway, she shows up fifteen minutes later with her hair pulled
back nice, and it's fine. She gets into it—the champagne, the
fire—it's perfect in her book, as far as I can tell. The touching
reunion I won't go into, but it's nice, we get a little tipsy, and
pretty soon things lead to things and we're naked and, well,
not our greatest performance, but it's good, I think; as things
bode, this bodes well. We're lying there after, drinking up the
last of it, and I lift my glass and say, "Zesty, with red stripes, a
gurgly wine," and this of course I find incredibly funny and so
I start giggling and can't stop, you know how that goes, I can't
stop for four minutes. And she's laughing a little, too; granted,
not uncontrollable like me, but it's not as if I'm laughing alone.
And finally I—we—settle down, and she looks at me and says,
"Hey, we insipid types got to stick together, right?"

So it's something I can live with, I figure. And I don't—I
repeat, don't—open up another bottle that night. Later, she's
in bed, I wait till the supermarket-log thing burns down, crum-

bling up in that blue flame it has, and then I throw my champagne glass into it, and it smashes—smash!—just like Count
What's-his-name, or whatever.

Bowling

253 was my high game. They couldn't believe it—Anna, Sybil.
"Beginner's luck!," as if we hadn't been playing off and on for
a year and a half already. I had a perfect game going until the
fourth frame. Anna—she regularly bowls in like the mid-200s—
even she couldn't touch me. She ended with a 239 or something. Afterward they all bought me a drink and said I was
possessed by the devil in charge of bowling.

All I can say is, thank God it was after the men stopped
coming. No, I'm kidding. Well, maybe. Ty would've been furious. Ty's way of bowling is to shoot the ball straight down
the alley at the head pin as hard as he can, and that of course
always leaves the impossible seven-ten split, which means you're
getting nines galore and you're lucky to break a hundred. He
hated that, but when I told him to aim for the one-three pocket
he'd just look at me and fume and say, "Roll the ball, Janet."
Sybil thinks that's why they quit coming—we started getting
better than them. One night after one game Harry tells us they're
sitting the next one out, and Ty and Lance and him go over to
the bar and order drinks. So, the four of us girls play, Elaine
looking over every two minutes to make evil-eye contact with
Harry, as if to say, "Don't you dare"—Don't you dare what,
none of us could ever figure out with those two, but you knew
it was "Don't you dare something." So of course they drink too

much, and of course Lance starts complaining about the price of electricity, just to get at Ty's goat, and of course Ty gets mad even though he knows it's just Lance being a jerk again. What a bunch! After two more games we've got to drive them all home, Sybil glorying with the I-told-you-so, and so we start coming by ourselves, just the four girls, and we all have a much better time from then on.

The 253 night was about five months later. Ty at home with his fish and his bottle of *vino*, as usual by that time. I never even told him about it. I came home, he was sitting in the glow of the aquarium, glassy-eyed, three-quarters of the way through a bottle of who-knows-what. What can you say in a situation like that? "Guess what, honey, I knocked down more of those stupid white pins than I ever did before"? When your husband's pie-eyed in front of a bunch of fish every night?

"A gutter ball." That's what Sybil always calls him. We used to do that, we'd get together on our Tuesday nights sometimes, have a few drinks, and start talking in bowling terms while she braided my hair. "Ty is a gutter ball in the alley of life," she'd say. Course I can laugh about it now. Well, then, too, I couldn't help it. I'd turn around and say, "When he strikes me, I can only say, Oh, spare me!" and of course we'd fall off her beanbag chairs onto the floor in hysterics. She even had a Bowling Theory of Life: Life is a tough split; you can either play it safe and go for the one pin, or else you can chance the narrow slice that'll either knock them both down or neither. She, she said, was trying for the slice; I had played it safe (and got a gutter ball anyway). This from the woman who had dated more losers than you can count on a calculator. Yes, she'd say, but I never married one.

She liked Angus, though. He'd come over all the time when it was just the four of us and flirt. He'd put his beer in one of those aluminum holes that nobody ever uses, sling his leg over the plastic chairs, and give us free games if we could guess what color underwear he was wearing (crass, I know, but we liked him for trying so hard). First time he came over we thought he was some kind of bull artist—this big, red-haired guy with freckles, name of Angus McNooney (right), owns a half-share of the alley. All true, though, every word he ever told us. At first we thought he might be good for Sybil, being the only unattached one of us, but she would just laugh at us. Red hair made her gag, she'd say.

It started one night—Sybil was home with smoker's bronchitis, Elaine had already stopped coming, and Anna said she didn't feel like bowling just the two of us. So I went alone. I didn't want to lose my game. Angus comes over before I've bowled even two frames. "So where's the entourage?" he says. I laugh. And he says do I want a drink, he'll make sure they hold the lane for me. I counted to five in my head, I looked up at him, and I say, Sure, who couldn't use a drink?

"Give Mrs. Steinbock anything she likes on my half of the house," he says to Henri, the bartender from I think Belgium, and so I order a Rob Roy, trying to make a joke, and he gets one, too, without cracking a smile, I can see he's as nervous as I am. That lovely round, muffled rumble of bowling going on behind us, I cross my legs and there are my feet all nicely done up in white socks and those wonderful comfortable blue bowling shoes Ty bought me when we were still coming together, and Angus all awkward like he never was before when there was the three or the four of us. We finished the first drink, talking about Sybil and whatever else we can think of, and finally he says, "You always smell like bread." I smile, and finally he smiles back, and there's a gurgle of pins being swept into the back of the machine, and he asks can he offer me another one, and I say—I really say it—"Don't I have to guess the colors any more?"

We'd go dancing. Angus prided himself on his Lindy, and he was pretty good, even with his limp. Sometimes I'd get tired and he'd dance with someone else. He looked awkward and graceful at the same time, like an ostrich trying not to step in something. Or we'd watch old movie musicals on the VCR in his private office at the alley. He cried—really cried—at the end of *South Pacific* once. "A lovely story," he said in that touch of an accent he has. We'd go out to movies also. Or bars. And everything for free. It seemed like Angus owned a piece of every business in Bergen County. Always in control, Angus. All he had to do was sign his name to get anything he wanted. Well, almost. He'd drive me back to pick up my car at the alley, and I'd kiss him good night, once. Then I'd drive home and make up bowling scores to tell to Ty.

The first time I left Ty, I knew I would end up at Angus's. I spent three nights on Sybil's beanbags and then moved in with him, Sybil covering for me in the Ty department. She, at least, was thrilled. President of the Angus McNooney Admiration Society. He had a college degree and some money, so she thought that he might just be good enough for me, despite the red hair. I wasn't ready, though. Even while I was taking down that green suitcase at home, I knew it wasn't time yet. I had never even been to Angus's apartment. He felt rushed, too, though he never would say so. He'd just rub the back of his neck and look at the floor. The first week we went out dancing or drinking every night—like we were still going out on our dates—but when I told him I couldn't live that way, he looked hurt and then annoyed. Or he'd tell me, one night getting out of the car, that my hair shined "lovely silver in the moonlight," and then, two minutes later, he's impatient when I can't get my new keys to work in his locks, and we argue. Meanwhile, Ty's showing up at the bakery every day after work, buying crullers one by one and eating them in front of me until I have to tell Audrey to stop selling him any. God, I was confused. Sybil said, "Stay, stay," but I wasn't sure. Why couldn't I do anything right?

Finally, one night we're in bed and Angus turns to me, very casually, and he tells me there's not enough nuance in my lovemaking. Not enough nuance. This from Mr. What-color-are-my-Jockey-shorts. I got out of bed and slept on the white shag rug on the living-room floor. And he didn't come after me. Next night he goes to the alley without me and I call Ty: "Put a log on the fire, honey; I'm coming home." And it was nice, really. He opened up a bottle of special champagne and we had kind of a romantic reunion. I had decided what I wanted. At least I could sit quietly with this man. I could make my own happiness. Next morning I rubbed flour into my hands and baked myself the biggest loaf of pure, unbleached whole wheat our oven could hold. Bun in the oven, bun in the oven.

Babies

They are merciless, you can quote me on that. I knew it was a bad idea from the beginning. Like we didn't have enough to handle already.

The guys out at PSE&G, they'd have babies, it would ruin

them. They'd be good for zero until ten, eleven o'clock—bags under the eyes you could pack ice into.

I thought we were in agreement on this point. One time we're out with this guy from work, Warren, and his wife, at this Italian place, Clams Casino or whatever. The third time they've left their kid with a sitter, so we figure they'll be relieved to get away from it all for a night. Wrong, of course. Warren's on about teething, for Chrissake, and What's-her-name's on about strained peaches. Abigail, Martha, some old-fashioned name like that. The kid's Brendan, after the old governor, they said. It's like everything had the kid's fuckin' name on it. The linguini reminds her of Brendan, and the waitress is six months pregnant, so God, we've gotta talk to the waitress for fifteen minutes about obstetricians before we can order. I told Janet later, I told her if they said aloud what the fuckin' summer squash reminded them of I was standing up and walking out of that place, fellow area supervisor or no, and she laughed. She *agreed* with me.

I mean, this is not a popular position, I realize it, but Jesus. And, I mean, Janet thought so, too. I thought she thought, at least. Then she hits me with it. Two months after she came back that time. We're at the table after dinner, polishing off the second bottle of I think it was Schloss Vollrads Kabinett, very easy on the way down, and we were feeling pretty good. It was a tough week for her at work, she said (as if nobody else has tough weeks? I mean, at least she brings home a couple of lemon pies and we get fat on her tough weeks). So, in sum, it was a Friday, and we were kind of celebrating the end of this tough week, I guess. She looked pretty ragged, actually, and once that week I woke up in the night and she was biting the pillow—I mean really biting it, like almost ripping the fabric—and she said it was something about some asshole customer, I don't know. So we're at the table and she drops this megaton thing on me. I'm, like, what the fuck? Are you serious? And she says, I think it will help us. I say, Like fuck (I'm kind of upset at this point), I say, I'm sorry, it can't be done, she says, It already has been, I say, Jesus fucking Christ. I am not a violent man. Janet has this thing, I mean, I'm no match for her. You've heard of the unstoppable force? Jesus f-ing Christ. So we have a baby.

I felt like I had nothing to do here. Janet's reading the books, seeing the doctors. I ask, Can I come along, she says, I'll just get bored, I say, Maybe I like bored, she says, Why, I don't want the kid anyway. And she's right. I'm sorry, what can I say? I'm some kind of monster, right?

All the time I know she's doing it for herself. Where am I in the picture? At the hospital the nurse comes out and says, "Who's Mr. Steinbock?" It takes me ten seconds to say, "Here."

First two months, the kid's got this vomit problem. Vomit everywhere, every hour of the day, we spend half my salary at the laundry. That's another thing—only one salary now, kiss the Moët goodbye for the next twenty-five years. I can't stay in the house some nights. I take up running, but my knee is kind of my Achilles' heel and all we've got is hard pavement to run on by us and who wants to have to drive to a park to jog a lousy two miles?

It's like two against one at this point. I'd get this idea that the kid waits until I'm holding him to vomit. I'm holding him once when Janet's in the kitchen warming up some formula. All of a sudden, the kid gets this, like, weird smile? He's looking up at me, and he's got this incredible grin on his face. So I take him out to the kitchen and say, "Jan, look, he's laughing at me, for Godsake." Then—blup!—white throw-up all over the front of my navy sweatshirt. Janet smiles then and takes him out of my arms. "Watch that the formula doesn't boil over," she says on her way to the bathroom.

It's unbelievable. Like the two of them had this secret plan. By the way, it's a boy. Benjamin is his name. Her idea. I never heard of a baby Benjamin in my life.

They live in Rockland County now—her and the kid—with some red-haired Irish guy she met at work or something. She lets me see him once every two weeks, but, Jesus. She says it's mine, she swears on a stack of Bibles it is. Fuck, it's got my nose, any jerk can see that. God knows what she'll tell him about me when he gets old enough.

I'm thinking, It's like, boom, two months after we're married, she's got me pegged. I hold Sybil responsible, partly. "I told you so" was all she ever could say to Janet. "The soul of a plumber," Janet told me once. Like she expected romance? You see what you want to see in things.

The baby was what did it. I think without Benjamin we could've, I don't know. Done it. Benjamin. I remember standing over his crib once, a few weeks old. There's this Bozo the Clown night-light by the crib, and that's all the light, and the kid's smelling like turpentine, God knows where from or how. He's finally asleep, after crying and vomiting for five, six straight hours, even the doctor doesn't know what the hell is wrong with him. I'm standing there, looking down at him, you know, when you're supposed to be getting all those warm paternal feelings? Well, all I can think is: "What the fuck is it with you? Where do you hurt, for Godsake?" Then, all of a sudden, his mouth goes, like he's sucking Janet's tit, up down up down, like he's saying something. Hey, Dad. Fuck off.

That's the thing about babies. They look like the bait, but they're really the trap.

Benjamin

Everyone was against it—Sybil, Ty, my mother—so I knew I was doing the right thing. And Angus wouldn't know, I decided, until I started showing. He'd see me getting bigger by the day, straining at the waist of the old bowling slacks, waddling toward the foul line. He'd think: God, thank God she left, I'd've been saddled with a middle-aged chubster with no nuance. Then, finally, one night, it would hit him: no carbohydrate binge this; no, this was serious; this was a seriousness of life he would never know. I wanted to see his red face turn redder when he realized it.

I knew what I wanted to do the day I went back to Ty. It happened that very night, in fact, during our little romantic tryst in front of the artificial log. I told him the thing was in, and it wasn't. Good old Ty—whatever else he is, at least he's fertile.

When I told him, he exploded—literally. I had expected some shock waves, but, God. You'd think I was telling him I wanted to leave again. He knocked half a bottle of wine on the floor, and for Ty that's something. He even tried to knock me on the floor, but, well. . . . It really must be frustrating for him. He yelled like a madman; he stormed around the apartment, throwing pillows against the wall. I stood over the stove, making tea. Nothing in the world was going to stop me. If Ty kicked me out, I'd go to Sybil's and have the baby on her beanbag couch.

Well, he got used to it. Never gave in, but at least stopped trying to break unbreakable objects against the wall. I never pictured us as the Lamaze type anyway. I hate pain, and having Ty along saying, "Push, honey, push," would've just annoyed me. So I went to Dr. Singh by myself. I'll take everything, I told him—laughing gas, Novocain, Gilbey's gin, whatever. Let's just get it done.

I bowled until the beginning of the seventh month (against doctor's orders). By that time it was like Janet the Planet sweeping past the points, throwing a little black moon out of orbit and into outer space. My game suffered. And Angus stopped showing up. The first few weeks he'd hardly let me play, buying me drinks and trying to talk me back into his BMW. I'd just listen to him and say nothing, thinking of the little baby I had growing inside of me. A few more weeks and he'd just watch us from a stool at the bar. I hurt his pride, Sybil said. She and Anna said we could all go to a different alley up on 9W, but I said it was fine where we were, he didn't make me nervous. Then he stopped being there. Business, was all Henri would tell me. Something about a share in another movie theater. I never saw him after the fifth month. Just after I began to show.

It was an easy pregnancy. Dr. Singh said I was born to be a mother. Best pelvic structure he'd ever seen. "Like wings poised to embrace the child," he'd say as he slid that cold stethoscope disk over my belly. Two weeks before my due date, he gave me a book of poems he'd written and published himself—*Gift of the Hummingbird*. "Like wings poised to embrace the child" was on page 34, in a poem about snow, I think.

God, I loved the way I looked then! It sounds sick, I know, but it's true. I just loved the way my belly got so round and tight, like that antique globe my father got for me in sixth grade. I never thought I looked fat, really; just very, very pregnant. Ty was a little leery, especially near the end. "Are you really supposed to get that big?" he'd ask me when I got ready for bed.

Benjamin was born on a Saturday evening. I remember thinking that it was my bowling night. Ty was in the shower when

I was first hit by "the prenatal drench and clench of determination" (that's *Gift of the Hummingbird*, page 44). I had to shout at him over the sound of running water: "It's time, Ty. Where's my crossword book to pack?" His hair was still wet when we pulled in at the emergency room. "I'll wait right here," he said. He was stepping back in the pink-and-blue maternity waiting room as they wheeled me through the swinging doors.

Anyway, it happened. I had a boy, Benjamin. Not too big; just about the size of one of Angel's special jumbo loaves of whole wheat. I saw his little blue scowl and knew right away that we'd get along just fine. "He looks mad," was all Ty would say, but when the nurse loaded Benjamin into his arms he looked up and smiled.

Next day I've got Benjamin for a breast-feed when Angus appears, dressed in a green three-piece suit I didn't even know he had. First time I'd seen him in months. "He hasn't got red hair and freckles, if that's what you're looking for," I said. He said nothing; just stared at me and Benjamin for a minute. "How'd you get up here anyway? Visiting hours are over." He lifted the greasy paper bag in his hand and said, "I brought you two slices of pizza." Then he smiled and gave little Benjamin a pat on the ass.

Ty took the week off from the plant and stayed home with me, but I could tell his heart wasn't in it. The guys from the bakery had sent over a white cake with chocolate icing, and Ty cutting it was like someone cutting the cake at a funeral dinner. He sliced right through the message—"Benjamin Steinbock: Born to Run"—without even a whisper of a smile. He's always been sad-looking, like his forehead was too heavy for his eyebrows to keep up. After three days I talked him into going back to work. I told him I could manage perfectly well on my own and that they probably needed him at work. He liked that. He said, "Well, if you're sure . . ."

When Angus started calling during the days, I really didn't want to hear what he had to say. I'd hang up on him, but he'd call back again and again. Finally, I'd talk to him, but only if he promised not to try to talk me into going back. I made him work, too; I'd make him guess what color the baby's eyes were today, and always said he was wrong, even when he wasn't. He'd tell me about this terrific house—"a great, comely place"—that he'd put a deposit down on—up in New York State, a three-bedroom near a lake—and I'd say "Oh." One day he sent over flowers and I had to flush them down the toilet before Ty came home. But in the end I went with him. I had to. Ty would never change; he would never even touch the baby unless I asked him to. So one morning Angus showed up with the BMW and we filled it with the baby stuff and a suitcase full of my clothes and we left. I left Ty a note: "I'm sorry I'm sorry I'm sorry." And I called him—the next day, from Rockland County, thirty miles away. He cried on the phone and asked me what it was I wanted from him. "Four years, Jan!" he shouted at one point. And I had to hang up on him; he wouldn't say goodbye.

Anyway, here we are now—the three of us in this big brick house in the woods. We've gotten over our rocky period. Angus still goes out a lot, from his alley to his theater to his this and that. Ben and I stay home. When he throws up, I clean it; when he cries, I hug him and make funny noises at him; no nuance required.

Ty comes to see us every other Saturday—when Angus is away, going over receipts at the alley. He drives up and sits with us in the living room for an hour, talking about things at work. Most times he wears a tie, something he never does, and I can catch a whiff of Skin Bracer on his cheeks. Then, after the hour, he looks at his watch and gets up from the chair. He gives Benjamin a kiss, and he bends that sad old face to me and we touch cheekbones. He drives away, and I say to myself, "That was the man that I married."

I wish him well, I really do. I hope someday he wins something—a sweepstakes or a contest or whatever.

He's still living in that apartment, drinking his bottles of expensive wine. He looks tired now when I see him. I ask him why and he says it's the puppies. He's bought himself a pair of tiny Labrador retrievers. They keep him up at night.

Evidence

There are new people next door. Three of them—a woman and
two men. The woman has long dirty-blond hair and very graceful ankles. She wears loose T-shirts and pastel-colored shorts
and big sunglasses that make her look like an owl, a pretty,
blond-haired owl. One man—the one I guess is her husband—
is tall and muscular with straw-colored hair and a dirty pipe
that he always seems to be filling with tobacco. I call them Sven
and Lena to myself—not their real names, certainly, but names
that seem to fit them. Their last name is Pedersen, or at least
that's what the fake-antique sign on their dock says—"The
Pedersens"—but they've never introduced themselves, so I can't
be sure. Maybe they found the sign somewhere and just liked
it. It's a big, solid oak sign with the letters burned in in elegant
script.

The other man is much smaller. Thin and wiry, with stringy
brown hair and an attempt at a mustache on his upper lip. He's
got the same squinted eyes as Sven, which makes me think they
must be related, but his face has a pasty look to it, and he hardly
talks at all except to answer a question. I don't have a real name
for him yet; I call him the Idiot Brother.

The name occurred to me after something he did just this

morning. I was sitting out in my lounge chair on the back terrace, which is where I usually go for an hour or so after breakfast to leaf through the new computer magazines and enjoy my view of the lake. About nine o'clock, I heard someone banging around the dock area next door. It turned out to be Idiot Brother; he was putting up the mast on the Sunfish to go sailing. Before he could get the centerboard in, though, he apparently decided that the wind was too chilly for the ripped T-shirt he was wearing, so he dropped what he was doing and ran back into the house for a jacket. He forgot, of course, to tie the line on the Sunfish, so by the time he came out again the boat was gone, sailing away by itself down the lake toward Beach 3, the line snaking behind it like a water moccasin. He stood on the dock watching it for a few seconds before the situation sank in: Boat Gone. "Damn," he said, kicking the edge of the dock before turning and sprinting back into the house. After a second or two, a much louder voice erupted from inside: "GOD DAMN!" Sven burst out the back door, ran down to the dock, cursed, and ran back. There was banging inside, more shouting, and then I heard them out front getting into the jeep. Not wanting to miss any of this, I ran through the house to the screened-in front porch and arrived just in time to hear Sven mutter ". . . the *stupidest* friggin' maneuver I ever heard," as he and Brother got into the mud-caked jeep. Lena was standing at the front door in a cardigan. "Leave him be," she said in a soft voice, her last word nearly lost in the sudden roar of the engine. Then the jeep pulled away in a spray of dirt and gravel. Lena, absentmindedly, raised her hand to wave good-bye.

I watched her for a few seconds from behind the dark screens. She looks about twenty-five, with very light, freckled skin and a way of standing with her arms crossed, each hand gripping the opposite elbow, as if she were trying to stop her body from falling apart. She smokes sometimes—long cigarettes. From what I can hear, she seems to have some kind of Southern accent.

I opened the screen door and walked out to the steps. "Hello," I said. She didn't seem to hear me. She just kept hugging herself in that way, staring down the road after the jeep, biting herself on the insides of her cheeks.

I've been in Highland Lakes for fifteen years now. Back when we moved in, it was a cheap place to live. That was before people decided that living on a lake was worth a ninety-mile round-trip commute to New York City. I was working in Paterson then and I liked to fish, so I thought what the hell. I paid seventeen thousand for the place; now I couldn't touch it for less than one-fifty.

I live alone, and have lived alone ever since my wife disappeared in October of 1977. She drove down to Oakland to go shopping on a rainy Saturday and never came back. The police thought at first that they had a few leads, but nothing ever panned out. They asked me a lot of questions, like whether our marriage had been happy. I told them it was. That wasn't a lie. Her name was Eleanor, and we had met at Tension Envelopes on Route 80, when I was helping them set up a new computer department. She liked to sail, and the only thing she knew how to cook was eggplant parmigiana. And now she's gone. Without a trace. That's all I'm going to say about Eleanor.

I free-lance as a computer consultant, which means that I don't work a lot of days, and that even on days I do work I can consult from the telephone in my little office at home. I have a spastic colon that keeps me in the house sometimes, so it's just as well that I don't have a regular nine-to-five. Consulting, at least at my level, doesn't pay too well, but I make enough to support me and my mother, who lives in Ramsey. I have about five thousand dollars in money-market funds and another eight in mutual funds. My father left me some stocks when he died—two hundred shares of Union Carbide and one hundred of IBM—and I myself have bought another hundred of Apple Preferred. I've got a Comet sailboat, a rowboat, a canoe, a Ford Fiesta, and Eleanor's old collection of Dresden china in a walnut cabinet in the living room. In five years the mortgage on the house will be paid, so I'll have that to fall back on in an emergency. And my mother is fully insured—Blue Cross, Blue Shield, and The Travelers Major Medical. In other words, we're covered.

I visit my mother every other Sunday. She lives in an apartment house that caters to old people—not a rest home, I would never send her to a rest home. The people take care of themselves at this place. My mother seems to like it. She has lots of acquaintances. They throw parties every week in the communal room overlooking the parking lot of the Swiss Chalet Restaurant. Sometimes the parties are on Sunday, and I sit with the old people in the communal room. We eat frosted white cake and drink wine and wear party hats—tiny crowns, sailor hats, firemen's helmets. It's not too bad, really. The old ladies make a fuss over me. They corner me at a table and make me listen to their stories of the days when Bergen County was the silk-weaving capital of the nation. When I tell them I work in computers, they cluck their tongues in wonder.

Other days I'm usually at home, talking to people on the phone or reading up on new developments. It's impossible to read too much about the computer business these days: things are changing so fast. Half my job is just keeping up with the industry so I can inform clients of their full range of options when they come to me about computerizing their operations. It's amazing to me how little people really know about what computers can do to help them. They still think of computers as number crunchers. I tell them that nowadays a computer program can diagnose diseases better than a doctor, and they look at me like I'm a traitor to the human race.

Actually, people are pretty ignorant in general about machines. And it's not just in the area of new technology, either. Most of my neighbors wouldn't know how to fix a lawn mower or a vacuum cleaner if their lives depended on it. They live surrounded by objects that are totally mysterious to them. Many of them probably think of electricity as some kind of magic.

I don't know, I guess I just think it's important to know how things work. Otherwise you're like the Amazon people who see a television and think that it's a bunch of little men running around in a box, shooting at each other with miniature pistols. On the other hand, I'm sort of an extreme exception when it comes to gadgets and machines. I've got every light in the house on a central computerized timer, for instance. And down on my dock I've set up this motorized winch to pull the boats up on the lawn when I'm done with them.

There's enjoyment—real enjoyment—to be had from knowing machines. My latest project, for instance: I bought a new RCA videocassette recorder with seven-day, four-event programmability, and I've hooked it to a movable satellite dish on my roof. The VCR is set up at the foot of my bed, and every night, just before I turn in, I program it to record broadcasts—news, movies, whatever—from all over the world. At two o'clock sharp, the machine trips lightly into operation. Sometimes I'll still be awake, and I'll hear it humming in the darkness, working away through the night, dutifully recording all those sounds and images for my eventual enjoyment.

That thought gives me pleasure; lying in bed, I can hardly suppress a smile.

The Pedersens, or whoever they are, showed up three weeks ago—Idiot Brother in the jeep and Sven and Lena in a battered old station wagon with the Sunfish tied to the roof. They pulled into the Hochheiser place next door on a hot Wednesday noon, trailing a cloud of exhaust fumes and dust behind them. From the very beginning, they looked like trouble; no sooner did Sven unfold himself from the front seat of the wagon than he started yelling at I.B.—something about a missed turnoff and a blue Cadillac with a U-Haul trailer. It took me a minute or two to notice Lena; she was just standing next to the passenger door of the wagon, saying nothing, staring off beyond the willow trees to the lake.

The Hochheiser place had been empty all winter, which was normal for that place. In my fifteen years on Rhododendron Island, I've never known anyone to live there for more than a few months at a stretch. Hochheiser himself is supposed to be some eccentric old man living in a nursing home in Vernon Valley. Ninety-three years old, with no next of kin. Refuses to sell and refuses to fix it up, so the place has been slowly collapsing for decades. It has dry rot and big holes under the eaves that the bats come through at dusk.

I suppose it would have been neighborly of me to go over there and introduce myself on that first day, but I didn't. I'm not a particularly sociable person, and besides, it's an unspoken rule among the dozen families on the island that permanents should not go out of their way to welcome renters. The Island Committee has been trying to discourage rentals for years now, primarily because some of the members don't approve of the type of people who tend to rent the Hochheiser place ("The Latest Hochheisers" is how Mrs. Ida Claiborne, Committee President, refers to them).

Nothing stops Franny Jaspers, though. Less than twenty minutes after the Pedersens' arrival, old Franny—our island maverick—came parading past my house with a Tupperware cake dish in her hands, a determined smile on her narrow, wrinkled face. "Good old Franny," I said aloud as she rounded the hedges. But then, two minutes later, she was on her way back, walking faster now, cake dish still in hand, looking like a cat who'd been pushed off a second-story windowsill. "Wait," I heard a woman's voice call. Franny stopped in front of my house and turned around. The blonde woman—Lena, as I had already begun to think of her—ran up to Franny. "I'm so sorry," I heard her say, but then her voice dropped and I couldn't hear anything more. The two of them talked for a minute or two, Lena shaking her head occasionally and drawing her fingers through her hair. Finally, just as Lena's voice was rising so that I could hear it again, Franny smiled and patted her on the shoulder reassuringly. She offered the cake; Lena took it, and kissed her shyly on the cheek before turning away. "Goodbye, dear," Franny called. And then the two of them headed off home in opposite directions.

I moved to the far windows on the front porch, just in time to see Lena stop and kneel down in front of the rhododendron bushes next to their front steps. She quickly slipped the Tupperware cake plate out of sight into the bushes. Then she got up, seemed to breathe deeply once or twice, and went back up the stairs and into the house, letting the screen door slam behind her.

It's Friday afternoon. Lena's out in the canoe now. I just caught a glimpse of her through the trees from the kitchen window. Heading for the middle of the lake. She's wearing something on her head—a straw hat, probably, to protect her skin against the late-afternoon sun. She has glossy, pearl-colored skin that's tight against her leg and arm muscles; it must be very sensitive to sun. I also noticed that she has a funny way of paddling; she pauses before every stroke, holding the paddle in the air a foot above the surface of the water, watching the drops fall from the blade into the lake.

This morning the breeze was blowing from behind the Hochheiser place. I was sitting on the back terrace drinking a yogurt shake, which is the only thing I can drink on days when the colon is acting up. The shake was strawberry, but the smell on the breeze was something else. I tried to identify it—something like sweat and mint tea and orange peels. After a minute or two, the smell was gone.

I spoke with her today for the first time. I was down pulling a few weeds in the bed next to the basement door when I heard a voice behind me say, "Hey, excuse me there." It was Lena, standing on their back porch, smoking. "Hi," she said, "I guess we're neighbors." She drew her hand through her hair. "My name's Greta Stokes."

I stood up straight and nodded. "Harold Finn," I said. "Welcome."

"What are those things, anyway? Those bushes," she asked, gesturing with her cigarette.

"Rhododendrons," I told her. "They're why they call it Rho-dodendron Island."

"Very pretty." She grabbed her elbow with her other hand then, and I noticed that she had a bandage around the thumb—a big bandage so white that it seemed almost to glow against her purple shirt.

"Did you hurt yourself?" I asked after an embarrassing silence.

"Oh, this," she said, holding the bandaged hand out as if she were inspecting her nails. "Just an accident. An occupational hazard."

"What kind of occupation?" I asked.

She gave me a suspicious look. "I make homemade wine once in a while," she said after a pause. Then, before I could ask what kind of injury you can get making homemade wine, she snapped her head toward her back door. "Oh, excuse me, the phone's ringing," she said, and moved toward the door. She pulled it open and was halfway through when she stopped and pulled back. "Nice to have met you, Mr. Finn," she said, smiling quickly and then disappearing into the house.

That was five hours ago. The only things I've seen since then have been a pair of men's legs moving around the yard beyond the oak trees at around two o'clock, and then Lena—Greta—in the canoe, disappearing from sight behind the Lawson place up-island.

When Eleanor and I were first married, we would entertain two or three times a month in our little two-bedroom house in Teaneck. Eleanor was very sociable, and I always liked cooking something unusual, like couscous or lamb korma or Brazilian black-bean casserole, for an audience. We enjoyed those evenings. We had some good friends in Teaneck—mostly neighbors, but also some people from Tension Envelopes, where she still worked in those days. Our dinner parties almost always ran until midnight or even later. All of us would just sit around the table after dinner, drinking Drambuie or Grand Marnier, getting a little drunk and laughing and telling stories. Eleanor would always sit across from me, and I'd watch her drink her liqueur. She had a very graceful way of holding the tiny glass, as if it were a conductor's baton; sometimes she would hold it against her cheek as she listened closely to what one of the guests was saying. She had this way of watching you as you spoke, as if what you were saying was the most important piece of news she had heard all day.

Anyway, there was this feeling I got—that we both got—when midnight would roll around and people would start leaving. We'd stand out on the porch together under the yellow insect-light, watching everyone get into their cars and start up their engines, rolling down their windows to call out a last thanks or a parting wisecrack, and I'd feel this sensation descending on me like a blanket—a kind of regret tinged with relief. I'd put my arm around Eleanor and pull her closer to me, pressing her shoulder against my chest. We were sorry to see them go. And yet, at the same time, we felt we could breathe easier. We were alone again. We had stepped out of our private lives for an evening, and now we had returned—our lives undisturbed, our secrets safe.

It's that kind of thing, I guess, that you miss the most—that easy intimacy. That weight against your chest at the end of the day.

I was sitting out last night, watching the moon, when I saw Sven and Greta on their dock next door. Greta was holding on to his shoulder while she stooped over to get a stone out of her sandal. Sven just stood there, watching what she was doing, letting himself be used for that moment as a fence post. Greta's hair swung back and forth as she shook the sandal. Neither one of them spoke. And then, after the moment was over, they both just turned and walked slowly back to the house.

During the police investigation of Eleanor's disappearance, the detectives would ask me questions like: "Did she take drugs?" or "Was she involved in any illicit activities?" "God, no, of course not," I'd answer. But they'd keep asking the same questions over again. Instead of going out and finding her, they'd just stay there in that room, looking at me hard and saying, "Are you absolutely sure?"

There were strange sounds coming from the Hochheiser place last night—the whirr of a vacuum cleaner, a woman laughing, and the repeated clang of something metallic against a pot or pan. Lights went on and off in different parts of the house. Someone got into the station wagon at about nine and drove fast down the island road and over the causeway to the mainland. Then there were more clanging sounds, the slam of a screen door. I heard Greta's voice saying "Peter?" in a loud whisper. A couple of lights went out.

Later, I was down in the basement, setting the timer for the clothes dryer. I saw a light go on in the Hochheiser kitchen. Their kitchen window is just about eight feet above and ten feet distant from my basement window, and since both were open,

I could hear everything that was going on. Greta was giggling quietly, and I could hear a man's voice saying, "Good show, good show," in a mock-British accent. "Stiff upper lip there, Greta," the voice went on. "No tears now, girl."

I had to see what was going on in that kitchen. I stuffed the rest of the clothes into the dryer, hit the button, and then ran up the basement stairs to my computer room, which has a window just across the alley from their kitchen. I was careful to leave the light off, so they couldn't see me, but I could see them almost perfectly. Greta was leaning back against a counter piled high with newspapers. She had her bandaged hand over her mouth, and she was shaking with laughter. Closer to the window, with his back to me, was Idiot Brother. He was dressed in a black racing swimsuit and nothing else. He held Sven's pipe in his hand, and he waved it back and forth as he said, "What ho, what ho, blimey," sending Greta into more waves of giggling. "Stop, Peter," she was gasping through her laughter, "you'll make me lose the egg salad." "Oh dear," he said, and scratched at his ass like a monkey. The skin on his long, smooth back looked slick with oil. Greta leaned forward and placed her hand on his wet shoulder. There was a look of complicity on her face. "He'd kill you if he knew you had it," she said.

I turned away from the window. A chill went through my chest, and then I felt the familiar acidic burning in my stomach. Moving away from the window, I went out of the dark room and down the hallway to my bedroom, on the other side of the house. I felt queasy, disgusted, as if it were my own body slathered with rancid oil. I kept thinking of Greta. Of that long, glazed back. And of poor Sven, away from home, unknowing.

I spent the next few hours in front of the television, surrounded by my warm laundry. I knew I wouldn't sleep. To settle my nerves, I watched an old Doris Day movie and a *National Geographic* special about sharks.

This morning I went over to the Hochheiser place.

I had seen Sven drive off in the jeep at eight-thirty, and Idiot Brother (or Peter, as I now knew him) was down at the dock washing the Sunfish, so I knew that Greta would be alone. I walked quickly down the road past the rhododendrons. The gravel under my feet, I remember thinking, sounded like a person chewing.

Greta seemed to hesitate before smiling when she saw me on the stoop. "Mr. Finn," she said as she pulled the screen door open to let me in. "Paying us a visit." I caught a whiff of rose perfume as I passed her into the living room.

The interior of the house was the same as it had been the last time I was in it—years ago, when I'd helped a family from Pennsylvania move in for the summer. Hochheiser's reproductions of old-master paintings still hung on the chipped stucco walls, and there were still one or two big stones missing from the fireplace. The rug was the same, too—a worn red-and-blue Persian-type with tiny deer bounding across it. In the far corner of the room, beyond a pile of dirty clothes, were a bunch of old hockey sticks and a collapsible bicycle.

"Can I get you something to drink?" Greta asked. "Coffee? Some of my wine?"

"I brought you something," I said stupidly, too loudly. I held up the bulb I had brought with me. "A bug light for the porch. I noticed you didn't have one. The yellow light doesn't attract insects."

She seemed genuinely pleased as she took it from me. "That's so nice of you, thank you." She admired the bulb for a second or two, turning it over in her hand. "So bugs can't see yellow," she said, as if this fact confirmed some deep, secret belief she had always held.

"Well, it's not a hundred percent effective," I started to say, but then drifted off. Greta had her hair pulled to the side so that it fell in a ponytail that just grazed the top of her shoulder. Her eyes, I noticed for the first time, were a kind of mud-brown color, streaked with black.

"So how about that coffee?" she asked after a moment.

"Well, I will try some of that wine you make, if I may."

She smiled. "A brave man. Have a seat and I'll be back in a minute."

I sat down in a worn, plaid-upholstered armchair while she went to get the wine. The cushions hissed under me, releasing a smell like alcohol. I rubbed my sweating hands together, trying to phrase in my mind what I wanted to say.

"It's my first batch of elderberry," Greta said as she returned to the living room with two glasses. "Mostly I make cranberry wine at home."

I took one of the glasses from her. "Where is home?" I asked.

"South Jersey. Chatsworth area."

She sat down in the chair across from me, smoothing her white skirt over her thighs.

"Will you be up here long?" I asked.

She grimaced comically. "Depends on who you ask. Me and my brother-in-law love it, but my husband doesn't. I think he's bored."

I nodded and stared at the condensation on my wineglass. "You husband seems to be away a lot," I said.

She paused a second before saying, "Oh, not so much, really."

I took a sip of the wine, which was bitter and very cold. "I guess something like that can put a strain on a marriage, being away a lot. Makes it that much more important for both people to, I don't know, trust each other. Communicate."

"Yes," she answered in a neutral tone. She seemed embarrassed, and flexed her fingers once or twice on her lap. "He's not really away so much at all," she said, shrugging.

"Well, even so," I began.

Then I heard the screen door at the back of the house sliding open. It had to be Peter, coming back into the house. I felt panicky suddenly, and sprang up from the chair. "I've got to go," I said quickly. "There's a call I forgot." I was determined not to let Peter see me.

Greta looked up at me as if I had spoken nonsense syllables.

"There's this business call," I said, almost in a whisper.

"Greta?" Peter's voice called out from the next room.

"Don't you want to meet Peter?" she asked, getting up and following me to the door.

"Another time, please." I pushed open the screen door. "Thanks for the wine," I said. But all of a sudden, I felt I couldn't leave. I turned back to her and grabbed her by the left wrist. "It's shameful, what you're doing," I hissed to her, petting her hand compulsively. "Just shameful. Your husband deserves to know his own wife!"

Greta's eyes narrowed, and she yanked her arm out of my hand. "You're sick," she said, pulling away from me with a snarl. Then I saw Peter's silhouette appear behind her in the doorway to the kitchen. I turned again, feeling the screen door slam shut behind me, and hurried down the steps.

* * *

Yesterday was Sunday. It was a hot, humid day, with high clouds and a smell of grass in the air. The surface of the lake was still and smooth, like a membrane. There were no sailboats.

At noon I got into my car and drove down to the apartment house in Ramsey to visit my mother. She wasn't feeling very well, she said, so we skipped the party in the communal room and had Sunday dinner up in her apartment. I made a rib roast with mashed potatoes and cauliflower. After dinner we watched *Pal Joey* on television.

I left Ramsey at about eight o'clock. There was some traffic on 23 on the way back, so it was already getting dark when I turned onto the causeway to Rhododendron Island. I was surprised to see a crowd of the neighbors gathered together in the road in front of Gene Heckler's place. I intended to pass them with nothing more than a wave. I slowed down as the figures parted in my headlights, but then Bill Danzig's round face appeared in a corner of my windshield and I heard a rapping on the roof. I stopped and rolled down my window. "You missed some excitement here tonight," Bill said.

"What excitement?"

"Down at the Hochheiser place," he said, stooping over and talking from under the arm he had propped on the roof. "That guy beat up on his wife. We had the police here and everything. I'm surprised you didn't pass the patrol cars on the road; they left just a few minutes ago."

"Franny went with them," Ida Claiborne added, looming over Bill's shoulder. Her forehead was glistening with sweat under the light of Heckler's driveway light. "To take care of the poor girl," she explained. "They said her arm was broken."

"Her arm," I said. I felt shaky. My hands on the steering wheel tightened. "He was so much bigger than her."

"No," Bill said, "the bigger one was the brother-in-law. The husband was the skinny one—Peter, I think his name was."

"The police think he hit her with something," Ida shouted. "An oar or something. In the left arm."

"We still can't figure out who it was that called the police," Bill said. "None of us did. We didn't hear a sound."

The headlights of a van coming around the turn behind me raked across the interior of my car. I saw my hand on the steering wheel go white suddenly, and then dark again as the van pulled into the Lawson driveway.

"Anyway," Bill went on, "we're having a committee meeting on Thursday night, if you can make it. To see if we can't prevent Hochheiser from renting the place any more. Or at least let us have a say-so in who he does rent to."

A moth flew in through the open window and collided with the headrest near my ear. "I'll try to make it," I said.

Bill rapped once more on the roof of the car and pulled away from the window. "Right here at Gene's," he said. "Seven o'clock."

I rolled up my window and started down the road. I pulled into my own driveway, about fifty yards down the road, and parked the car. It was quiet when I got out; all I could hear were the trill of crickets in the rhododendrons and the irregular lap of the lake against my dock. Every once in a while, heat lightning flashed silently in the dark sky, throwing the treetops intermittently into silhouette.

Next door, the Hochheiser place was dark.

It was later that night that I took a walk down to the undeveloped lot at the north end of the island. The moon was about half full, and when it broke free of the clouds, I could see my way fairly well through the bushes down to the water's edge. There's a little cove with a gravelly beach down there, and for some reason all of the junk that's ever been lost in the lake washes up on the gray and white stones on one side of it. Sometimes the beach can be a mess, littered with old aluminum cans, pieces of rotted rope, candy wrappers, broken oars—any kind of trash imaginable. One time, the day after a fifteen-year-old girl had drowned off Beach 4, I found a maroon barrette there with a few strands of red hair tangled in the clasp. I thought for a while that it might have come from the drowned girl, and I even kept it for a few days, thinking I might give it to the mother one day. But then I found out that the girl had been a brunette, and that she had been wearing a bathing cap at the time she drowned.

I sat down on a boulder and looked out across the lake, at the play of dock lights on the water. Every once in a while, a bat, hugging the surface in search of mosquitoes, would silently skim across the wavy path of one light.

I used to go to that place all the time back in 1977, just after Eleanor's disappearance. I used to try to feel her presence there. It actually worked sometimes; I never talked to her or anything weird like that, but just pretending to be with her made me feel better. But I stopped after a while. It started to seem stupid and corny to me, and it became harder to conjure her up, especially after all the police interviews.

But last night, the night Greta Stokes was beaten up by her husband, I didn't even think about Eleanor as I sat on the boulder. Eleanor was gone. Ten years had passed, and I had already been through all that—the wondering, the not knowing. That case was closed.

It's Wednesday night now, three nights later. The weather has continued hot, the sky broken only by a few strands of cirrus to the south and southwest.

I called my mother today. She sounded very depressed. She said her ears hurt.

The Hochheiser place is still dark. I haven't seen or heard anybody there since Sunday, but the jeep is gone from the driveway and the Sunfish has been pulled up from the dock to the side of the house. Maybe Sven came when I was gone one afternoon. I've been away from the house for a couple of hours every day, overseeing a job in Wayne; the owner of a big restaurant down there wants to computerize his inventory; he hasn't got the vaguest idea how to go about it.

I've done my monthly accounting for July. A slow month (the summer months always are), but I'm still riding on a two-hundred-hour consulting job with Epoch Hardware this past spring, so I'm not worried. My net worth as of July 31 is $186,500, including a conservative estimate of the value of the house (minus outstanding mortgage) but not including my possessions (car, boats, computers, appliances).

I was down at the cove again tonight. I went there to think about what I would say at the Island Committee meeting tomorrow night. Ida Claiborne and Gene Heckler have been known to steamroll their own proposals through the committee with hardly a pause for a vote; they can be pretty formidable when their indignation is raised. Actually, I'm not sure what I really think about the question of renters at the Hochheiser place, so I went to the cove to decide. One part of me thinks Ida and Gene are right, and that we *shouldn't* allow another set of Hochheisers to move in and upset the neighborhood; another part of me thinks that old Hochheiser has the right to do whatever he wants with his own house.

It's a tough question. I spent an hour at the cove debating with myself about it, but I ended up not deciding anything. I wasted my time, I guess. The only thing I have to show for the hour is a fierce headache and a red plastic sandal that washed up at my feet as I stood there.

The Canonization

The piano in the dining room is out of tune. You hit an A and it plays a G. You hit a G and it plays a G.

This fact thrills my younger brother, Pete. He hasn't had a lesson in weeks. Mr. Vidivic, his teacher, won't set foot in the house until the piano is tuned. But Mr. Digby, the tuner, is in Rumania visiting his dead wife's family. We called Mr. Digby's kids, but they aren't sure when he'll be back. They say they last got a card from him two weeks ago, from the Mediterranean coast. I looked up Rumania in my atlas. It doesn't have a Mediterranean coast. So the piano stays untuned.

Meanwhile, as my brother runs free, I have to work. I have this English assignment that's giving me nothing but trouble. It's a paper on "The Canonization" by John Donne. The poem seems a little pornographic to me, but Mrs. Anderson says it's about God. That's the only hint she'll give me. She says I'm her best student and she's counting on me to figure it out on my own. There's this one line in it I really like: "We can die by it, if not live by love." I'm trying to focus in on that line in my paper. It seems to make sense—at least more sense than something like "The phoenix riddle hath more wit / By us: we two being one, are it," which is a total mystery to me. This is what it means to be somebody's best student.

I thought of asking my grandmother about the poem. My father says she was a poet in her youth. Her love poems to my grandfather were printed in the Vienna newspapers. I don't think she knows much about English poetry, though. My grandmother will be eighty-two in February, and she lives downstairs in our refinished basement, where we can all look after her. She's my father's stepmother, born in Austria, and she still speaks with a heavy accent. "Rolph" she calls me, instead of Ralph. There are these thick, creased rings around her neck, and she seems to grow a new one every year, like a tree.

Every day after school for the past week, my grandmother has sent me out to the corner deli for milk. She likes to let me keep the change. She's actually been sending me out for milk for years, but only recently has she gone overboard. There are five unopened quarts lined up on the top shelf of her Frigidaire. Some of them are beginning to smell.

My mother tries to stop me from buying any more milk for her. "Tell her to finish what she's got already," she says, "or remind her that you went just yesterday. She forgets if she doesn't look in the refrigerator." My grandmother *is* forgetful. And she has something wrong with her leg that keeps her in bed most of the time, so sometimes she doesn't get to the kitchen for days on end. But I think she hasn't really forgotten what's in her Frigidaire. I think she knows, and I buy the milk anyway. If somebody wants something, I figure, we owe it to them not to second-guess them. Who knows why somebody wants something anyway? So I add the new quart to the lineup and let my grandmother thank me. I hold out the change to her, and she closes my hand around the coins. Then she lifts it to her cheek and holds it there for a minute. She has rough, whiskery cheeks. When she kisses me, I can hear her cheek rasping against the collar of my jacket.

"Do you know John Donne, Grandma?" I asked her this morning.

"Your little friend from across the street, na?" she said, her pale-blue eyes vibrating at me. My grandmother thinks I'm still eight years old.

"He's a poet, Grandma. He wrote love poems, like you."

"Love poems!" she said, and then chuckled, making the bed squeak under her.

"Didn't you write love poems when you were young?"

"*Ach, Gott,*" she said, waving the idea away. Then she turned her eyes on me again. "I should write a love poem for my little Rolph, na?"

She was holding out her hands to me. I let her grab me and kiss me loudly on the ear.

That's when my mother called me from upstairs. All of a sudden, my grandmother's face went dark. She leaned back against her pile of flowered pillows and closed her eyes. For a second, she looked dead to me.

"Ralph?" from the top of the stairs.

My grandmother's lips moved. "Mama's calling now," she said, without opening her eyes. Her lips were almost white. "She vants you."

There was a note for me taped to the refrigerator when I got home from school. It was from my mother: "Ralph: Times is in the den; pay special attention to article on page A-23."

My mother has started me on this new project. She makes me read *The New York Times* every day after school. Reading it is a little scary for me sometimes, which makes my mother nod her head in satisfaction. It's not bad, she says, to be a little scared by things like nuclear warheads and famines and international tensions. But it's not those things that bother me, really. It's the little things. Once I read about people in the South who eat dirt. Nobody makes them do it. They just eat it for their own pleasure. There's a kind of red river mud that's supposed to be especially desirable. Smooth and fine-grained, said one woman in the article. This was disgusting to me. Nobody should eat mud, not even animals.

The paper is full of things like that—people who dress themselves up in dollar bills, one man in Montana who spent his entire life trying to get on TV game shows. I try to skip articles like that. People should have more dignity, I think. I spend more time on the articles about Russia, since I know that those are the ones my mother will ask about.

I thought it was probably another superpower article that she wanted me to pay special attention to today. But when I went to the den and opened to page A-23, it was an article on Alzheimer's disease. She had bracketed it in red ink. ''Everyone has a responsibility to know what's going on,'' she had written on a stick'um clinging to the margin. ''Ignorance never helped anybody, which is why you've got to explain to your grandmother about the milk. Her mind will just go completely if you let it.''

My mother is very good at this—themes, wisdom, finding lessons for everyday life in something like a newspaper article. She was probably great at English when she was in eighth grade. Of course, I've thought of asking her about ''The Canonization,'' but I know what she'd say. "What do *you* think it means?" she'd ask, wiping her hands on a dishrag and staring at me with those watchful eyes. My mother and Mrs. Anderson have a lot in common.

I glanced through the article on Alzheimer's disease. My mother had underlined certain phrases—"memory loss," "cell death," "abnormal brain waves"—but somehow I couldn't bring myself to read the piece. None of this had anything to do with what was happening to my grandmother. Anybody could see that. My grandmother sent me out for more milk because she wanted me to get it for her. It made no difference how many quarts she already had.

I threw the newspaper in a chair and went downstairs to my grandmother's apartment. There was no answer to my knock, so, very quietly, I opened the door and went in. The place smelled like eucalyptus and garlic. Around her neck my grandmother sometimes wears old rags that she's soaked in a boiled solution of eucalyptus leaves and garlic cloves. She says that they help prevent sore throats, but I think they just make her smell good. Every time I go into an Italian restaurant or eat a cough drop, I think of my grandmother.

She was lying on the bed under a pile of blankets, which rose and fell as I watched. I tiptoed to the other side of the bed to see if she was awake. She wasn't. Her creased lids were shut hard over her eyes, and the right side of her face looked smashed against the pillow. Her mouth was open, and there was a tiny river of spit running down from it to the edge of the pillow.

I looked at the deep wrinkles in her face. "We can die by it," my mind said, "if not live by love."

Upstairs, my brother started playing the piano—"Doctor Zhivago," with all the notes just slightly off.

* * *

The due date for my paper is getting closer. No extensions, says Mrs. Anderson, because good students don't need extensions. I've written one line so far: "John Donne was born in 1572 to a family of Roman Catholics in a time of anti-Catholic feeling in England." Twenty words.

Of course, there's a simple solution to my problem—the Englewood Library. Louis D'Angelo says there's a section on John Donne as long as your arm. But Mrs. Anderson made me promise—no secondary sources. There's no joy in it, she says, unless you decipher it yourself. That's fine, but I don't seem to be getting anywhere with the poem. "When did my colds a forward spring remove?" reads one line. I understand all the words, but I still don't get it.

And meanwhile, the Englewood Library stands on its little hill, containing the answer.

Not that I could get to the library today even if I decided to give in. I'm grounded. My mother caught me going to the deli again for my grandmother yesterday. She stopped me just as I was heading downstairs with the quart of milk in a brown paper bag. "Until you can behave responsibly like an adult, Ralph," she said, blocking the stairs, "you will be treated like a child." She took the milk out of my hands. "This will be in our refrigerator up here until you decide to tell the truth down there," she said. Then: "It's for your own good, Ralph."

She's decided that she herself will say nothing to my grandmother about all of this. It's become my responsibility. It will be a strengthening experience for myself *and* for Grandma, my mother claims.

"It's easy to be unfair to your mother," my father said carefully when I complained to him about it. "But without someone like her, you know, I'd never have kicked the booze." It's true, my father used to be drunk all the time. He'd come up to my bedroom to kiss me good night, and I could smell the sweet bourbon on him before he even got through the doorway. That was five years ago. He doesn't touch a drop any more. He doesn't come up to kiss me good night any more, either.

My grandmother fell down yesterday. I was at school. She was all alone when it happened.

My mother found her at around noon, crumpled up on the carpet at the foot of her bed. Her arm was bent under her body, my mother told me, and her ankle was swollen. She was "conscious but disoriented." After calling the ambulance, my mother lifted her to the bed and then asked her questions to find out if she had had a stroke. By the time the paramedics arrived, my mother had already decided that my grandmother had only fainted. The paramedics agreed. They were gone after a few minutes, leaving behind an ice pack for my grandmother's ankle.

When I got home from school, my mother told me what had happened. "It's probably not anything serious," my mother said. "She may just have got up from the bed too fast, but she's frightened. And she wants to see you." I was downstairs before I had even taken off my coat. My grandmother was spread crooked across the bed, her feet dangling over the side. Violin music was playing on the radio on her night table. She was staring at the wall as I came in.

"Grandma?" I said.

She turned and looked at me. Her mouth was a tight line, surrounded by wrinkles. "I don't vant this, Rolph," she said, holding out the blue-and-white plastic ice pack. "You take it avay, please."

I stepped over to the bed and took the pack from her. It was doughy and cool in my palm. "Your ankle is OK now?"

"The bag makes me too cold," she said. "Hot, not cold, is right. Hot makes the leg heal."

This seemed wrong to me—why did the paramedics leave the ice pack if it wasn't the right treatment?—but I wasn't sure. "I can get you the heating pad. Upstairs."

"Mama says no," she whispered, flashing her eyes up toward the ceiling. "The doctor is saying tomorrow mit the pad." She looked away from me toward the casement windows. "They don't vish for me to be healty," she said quietly.

I looked down at her ankle. It was thick and interlaced with puffy blue veins. It looked like it hurt. "I'll be right back," I said to her.

I found the heating pad in the linen closet on the second-floor landing. "Doctors don't know everything," I told myself, and then grabbed the pad. I hid it under my sweatshirt and, walking quietly past the open kitchen door, went downstairs again to the basement. *"Ach, Rolph,"* my grandmother said in a loud whisper, *"du liebes Kind."*

"I'll set this up for you here," I said. I put the heating pad down on the mattress next to her and then crawled under the bed to plug it in. It was dark under there, and dusty and smelly. I had to force myself to go all the way under. When I got to the wall, I saw an old nightshirt balled up in the corner. I reached out my hand to grab it, but then I saw the dark-brown stains all over it. I pulled my hand back and felt a gag rising in my throat.

My grandmother must not have been able to reach her bathroom one day. She must have pushed that nightshirt under the bed so that no one would find it. She must have been so ashamed.

The bed creaked above me. "Rolph?" my grandmother's voice, muffled by the mattress, asked.

I quickly pushed the plug into the wall socket and then backed out from under the bed. "It's on. I'm setting it to medium." I turned the dial and then set the pad down on her lap. I tried not to look in her face. "I have some homework to do now, Grandma," I said.

"Rolph!" she called out as I turned away. Her eyes were on me again. "I can't bend."

I swallowed. "I'll wrap it for you," I said. Stepping back to the bed, I took the heating pad in my hand. It was already warm. "Let me know if this is too hot for you," I told her. Then, with my other hand, I lifted her foot. The skin was white and damp, and the foot was heavy. I tried to stop my mind from thinking of it as a big dead fish in my hand. Hurrying, I slipped the pad under her ankle and placed her foot carefully back down on the mattress. "I'll put a pillow here to keep it pressed down on the top of the ankle," I said, "and then I'll cover you with the blanket. That will help to keep the pillow in place." I watched my hands as I arranged the bedding. When I finished tucking the blanket under her, I looked up.

My grandmother's eyes were wet. She said something in German that I didn't understand. Her arms were stretched out toward me—like an octopus's tentacles in a cartoon.

I felt like crying. Her fingers were shaking in midair. The gag in my throat changed to a sob, and I took one step forward.

* * *

I handed in my paper for school. It ended up being much shorter than it was supposed to be, but it was the best I could come up with. Donne is supposed to be one of the hardest poets anyway. Next month we'll be doing John Milton, who Louis D'Angelo says is much easier. Here's what I wrote:

John Donne was born in 1572 to a family of Roman Catholics in a time of anti-Catholic feeling in England. That fact explains a lot. People were probably always bothering him about religion and such things, when all he really wanted was to be left alone so that he could love his girlfriend the way he wanted to.

I say "love his girlfriend," but it's really more than that. The poem may seem pornographic, but as many insightful critics have pointed out, it's really about God, God in the broad sense, that is. If you love your girlfriend, or whoever is the object of your love, you're loving God in a way. There's something sacred about it and it shouldn't be interfered with. "For Godsake hold your tongue, and let me love," says the first line of the poem. And it really is "for Godsake" that Donne is saying that.

The problem, really, is other people—the ones that Donne is talking to in the poem. They go on and on about so-called serious things, telling you what's good for you and what you should do. But Donne wants no part of that: "With wealth *your* state, *your* mind with arts improve," he writes (italics mine). Go ahead and improve yourself; just leave me alone with my love; what business is it of yours? "Alas, alas, who's injured by my love?" (line 10).

In conclusion, people are dying all the time. They don't

need their characters built; they need to go out with some dignity; they need love. That, I think, is what Donne is trying to express in this poem.

That's all I had time to write. It was a lost cause from the beginning. I left wide margins and actually put two and a half spaces between lines instead of only two, but the paper was still about half the assigned length. Mrs. Anderson will probably be disappointed. I guess it doesn't really matter. Louis D'Angelo says that colleges never look at your grades from junior high school anyway.

Since handing in the paper, I've been reading some of the other John Donne poems in the textbook. They're very good—hard, but good. It gets me to thinking: maybe I'll be a poet when I grow up. I could write love poems like Donne. Like my grandmother, too.

My parents announced at dinner last night that there would be a family meeting after the dishes were washed. I knew that something important was up. My mother never calls a family meeting lightly.

After we finished eating, we all did our Thursday-night jobs. Pete went down to bring up my grandmother's tray, I cleared off the table, and my parents washed and dried. Pete and I finished first, so we went into the living room to wait until my parents were through. Pete sat at the piano and I stood above him, watching the keyboard. He had figured out a way to play "Jingle Bells" so that it almost sounded right. The only thing was, he was hitting all the wrong notes. The piano was so out of tune that he could play nonsense on the keyboard and the piano would play something that sounded like "Jingle Bells."

My parents looked very serious when they walked into the room. They asked my brother and me to sit on the couch so that they could have the armchairs across from us. We all sat there for a minute in silence. My father stared at a patch on the arm of the couch, but my mother looked us straight in the eye, from me to my brother and back again. I felt like there was something cold and alive fidgeting in my stomach.

"Bill?" my mother said without taking her eyes off of us.

My father cleared his throat. "Kids," he began, "as you know, your grandmother had kind of a nasty fall the other day."

Oh God, I thought, I knew it was going to be something like this.

"She's getting very old," he went on, but then he went silent and looked down at his wingtip shoes, as if they would give him some cue to go on.

"Your father and I have given this a lot of thought," my mother said. She leaned forward and rubbed the back of one hand with the other. "We've decided that we're not able to give her the attention she needs at this stage in her life. You kids are at school all day, and your father's at work. I can't be here all the time to check on her. Next time she faints—and I think there will be a next time—I may be out grocery-shopping and not be back here for hours." She breathed deeply. No one else in the room seemed to be breathing. "So we've decided," she went on, "to find a place for her, a nursing home where she won't be alone so much. There's a very nice one in Hackensack. Dad and I think she'll be happy there."

"Yes," my father said softly.

My mother leaned back again in her chair. "But in this family, we discuss things, and that's why we're having this meeting. If either of you wants to say something, we're here to listen."

My brother shifted noisily on the couch next to me. I looked up and realized that all three of them were staring at me. "Ralph?" my mother asked.

The thing in my stomach was dead now. I felt like I had lived through this entire scene before, and that I knew what part I had to play. I had to be the grown-up boy, sensible and responsible. My mother had written the script beforehand. "I guess you're right," I said slowly. "She's really old."

I saw my father's body sag in relief. My mother looked satisfied. "Good," she said. "We'll discuss it with Grandma, of course. We don't want her to do anything she doesn't want to." She put her hands on her knees and then got up from the chair. The rest of us followed her lead. "I think it's best for all of us," she added.

Then, suddenly, it all hit me. "No, this is terrible!" I shouted, and I pushed my brother back down onto the couch so hard that he almost bounced all the way up again. I turned to my mother. Her face was tight. There were ropes standing out in her neck. "This stinks, goddamn it!" I shouted even louder. Then I pushed past her and headed for the door to the basement.

"Ralph, you're being foolish," my mother said steadily from behind me. "You can only hurt her now."

I almost tumbled down the steps as I ran. The hallway was dark, but I moved through it fast, banging bookshelves with my shoulder. My grandmother's door was closed. I felt for the doorknob and, without knocking, opened it.

My grandmother was there, right in front of me in the kitchen, leaning on her cane. The room was dark except for the bright light from the open refrigerator. She looked like she was standing in a spotlight. There was an open quart of milk lying on the floor in the triangle of light. Clotted white liquid was pouring out of the spout toward my grandmother's feet. The air smelled sour and thick.

"Rolph," my grandmother said to me. Her face was scared in the cold, white light. "So much milk," she wailed, "so much milk, how could you?"

Housesitting

At night, Lisa liked to stand near the pool in the backyard, just within the blue halo of the underwater floodlights, and watch the ripples of light splinter against the outside wall of the living room.

The house seemed huge to her, ridiculously huge; its spaciousness fascinated her. Before, she had always lived in small, sensible places that she had shared with other people—her parents, a roommate, a boyfriend. But she was free of that kind of crowding now, and she could almost feel her freedom like a physical sensation, of trimness and weightlessness. Every evening, when she returned from the library to that dark mountain of a house, she would change quickly into her bathing suit and walk barefoot out to the pool. Without pausing, she would dive into the cool, iridescent water and skim silently along the bottom to the drain at the deep end. There she'd stop, make all her muscles go limp, and let herself rise slowly to the surface—like an enormous thundercloud, she thought, dense and light at the same time, looming up over a horizon of black trees.

The house belonged to Professor Whitelaw, her adviser in the graduate math department. It was a rambling Tudor mansion, standing among red maples about thirty yards back from the road. Professor Whitelaw had asked her to live there for the months of July and August, while he and his family attended conferences in Europe. He had refused to accept any rent from her, stipulating only that she pay her own utilities and that she try her best to keep his wife's African violets alive in the second-floor sunroom.

Lisa had been living there for five weeks. She no longer felt dwarfed by the house, as she had at the beginning; in fact, she now liked to think that a kind of benign aura clung to the walls of those shadowy, high-ceilinged rooms. Their dry, slightly fusty smell had become familiar to her, like the endearingly sour breath of a lover. She could sink into a deep leather sofa in the den, or press her face against the cool brass fittings in the master bathroom, and imagine that she was somehow healing herself. And there were books everywhere, all sorts of books—facsimile editions of Shakespeare, austere clothbound translations of the German Romantic poets, well-thumbed paperbacks with titles like *Murder at the Parsonage* or *Dream of the Red Chamber*. She liked to read them in the den at night, curled up in the wing chair next to the green-shaded lamp, a bowl of wet plums and nectarines on the table beside her.

She slept in the master bedroom, at the end of the upstairs hall. It was the brightest, airiest room in the house, with a high canopied bed, white lacquer furnishings, and sheer lace curtains that floated and twisted in the breeze. On either side of the bed were windows that overlooked the back patio and the pool. She never closed these windows. Through them, she could hear the steady croon of the water filter every night before she fell asleep.

There were times, of course, when being in the house sad-dened her—when she was handling the trophies in the billiard room, or wiping the dust from the matted leaves of Mrs. White-law's violets. This wonderful house, after all, was not hers; she was borrowing it, just as she borrowed books from the library. There was a due date to be observed. The Whitelaws would return again on September 3, and the house would be taken away from her.

More often, however, she enjoyed the slightly disquieting sense of being in someone else's territory. After a few initial scruples, she began—timidly at first, more brazenly later—to examine the contents of boxes and closets throughout the house. She flipped through the professor's suits, shirts, and ties in the bedroom closet, smiling involuntarily when she came across something wildly out of character: a loud yellow-and-green Hawaiian shirt with palm trees, parrots, and the word "Ja-maica" printed haphazardly all over it. In Mrs. Whitelaw's bu-reau she came across a sexy lace teddy that seemed never to have been worn. Lisa held it against her own body, but then, a chill of guilt running through her shoulders, she folded it up neatly and placed it carefully back in the drawer.

One evening—just after a thunderstorm that had blown rain into the south-facing windows, soaking all the curtains—she took down some photo albums from the den bookcase and settled herself in the wing chair. As she leafed through them, stopping at pictures of other people's weddings, graduations, and parties, she felt suddenly uneasy. These might have been anyone's pictures, she thought, even her own. People smiled or grimaced at the camera, held up drinks, put their arms around each other's shoulders, just as they did in the pictures in her own albums. Even the settings seemed the same—cloudy, washed-out beaches, shady college lawns, church steps. All of those people could have been her own friends, or the friends of her parents. The realization made her feel slightly ill.

Then, on the last page of one of the albums, she came across a picture of herself. It had been taken the previous September, at the Whitelaws' annual math-department barbecue. In the picture she was standing next to a redwood picnic table, holding a glass of iced tea to her lips and smiling, as if she were amused by the ice cubes in her drink. She wore her long straw-colored hair pulled back from the temples, and her hand—the one without the glass—was resting on her hip with an almost arrogant casualness.

What drew her attention in the picture, however, was the figure standing next to her. It was Phil Egan, the man she had been living with at the time of that barbecue. He stood next to her, a dripping glass of beer in his hand, his head turned sideways from the camera to watch something going on beyond the frame. She was astonished at how young he looked. The skin on his cheek seemed as flushed and smooth as a boy's.

Her face was suddenly hot. Had she really made a fool of herself, she wondered. There had of course been the open needling from the other graduate students—Phil had only been a junior when they first started dating—but she had never really imagined how the two of them actually looked together. Somehow in her own pictures the difference in their ages hadn't seemed so extreme.

Lisa removed the picture from the plastic slot in the page and looked at it more closely. It was the first time she had really looked at his face in the five months since he had left her. His departure had come as a total surprise to her; one morning he had simply told her that he was dropping out midsemester to spend the summer in Copenhagen, learning Danish. She thought he was making a joke at first; things had been working out so well with them, she thought.

Now, alone in her professor's enormous house, she replaced the picture in its slot and closed the photo album in her lap. The whole affair with Phil seemed so strange to her, as if she had not really lived through it at all. This fact disturbed her, perhaps even more than the fact of Phil's leaving had disturbed her. She felt almost thankful to Phil these days: his going had helped her in some respects, she thought—had made her more durable and solid and watchful. Like a wolf, she would tell herself, trying to believe it: alive, solitary, and maybe just a little bit noble.

Lisa turned her head away toward the window. A branch of red maple was visible just outside, its bark almost pale in the dim light from the patio. She watched as big drops of rain fell from its leaves, dropping silently to the warm slate below.

There were lights on in the house one night when she came back from the library. Lisa stopped just inside the stone gateway and watched for a few moments, hugging her books to her chest, afraid to go inside. The Whitelaws weren't due back for another three weeks. No one else had a key that she knew of. She leaned back against the gateway, pushing her shoulder blades against the hard rock.

Finally, she decided to investigate. She placed her books down on the slate walk and circled toward the side of the house. Light was coming from a small window that looked into the living room. She slipped through a gap in the yew bush and then made her way to the window, pressing herself against the wall just out of reach of the stiff branches. The light from the window reflected off the back of the bush, and for a moment she felt as if she were entering a tiny white room.

When she got to the window, she stopped and breathed deeply. The moisture from the afternoon's rains crept into the soles of her canvas shoes, now caked with ink-black soil. She looked down at them for a few seconds to prepare herself before craning forward to peer through the glass.

The living room seemed slightly unfamiliar to her from this vantage point. There was a white sweatshirt draped over the sofa, and a chair had been moved across the room to a position directly in front of the television. A man in a T-shirt and cut-off jeans—a teenager—sat in the chair, with his legs up on the television trolley. The blue light of the television flickered on the dull surface of his thighs.

She recognized him immediately as Carl Whitelaw, whom she had met several times at the Whitelaws' barbecues. He was supposed to be in Europe with his parents. But there he was, splayed out in front of her, casually occupying the living room. Lisa watched him through the glass and felt suddenly that another part of her life was ending abruptly, before she was ready to let it go.

She shifted her weight, and her shoes sank farther into the spongy soil. It was several minutes before she turned from the window and made her way back out through the yew bush.

"It's raining in New Orleans" was the first thing he said to her when she entered the living room. He had barely looked away from the television as he said it. The weather channel was on; wispy clouds crept across an outline of the United States on the screen. He had not even put his legs down when she walked in.

Lisa stood slightly behind and to the left of him, refusing to move into his line of vision. "Is there a problem?" she asked. "Why aren't you in Brussels?"

Carl swung his legs down from the trolley and turned toward her. His hair was damp and it hung down on his forehead in tiny quills. "My best friend's mother died," he said. "The funeral's on Saturday."

"I'm sorry," she said as a reflex. Then: "Why didn't you call, warn me you were coming?"

Carl stood up suddenly. "That," he said as he crossed the room in front of her to the telephone, "is exactly what I tried to do." He pushed away some newspapers and revealed the answering machine, its tiny red call light blinking furiously. "One, two, three calls, at three different times of day."

"Oh," she said. She realized that she had not checked the machine—which she had vague philosophical objections to—in several days.

"Anyway," he went on, "I'm sorry about it, but it'll only be for five days or so. I guess I *could* stay at my friend's—"

"No, of course not!" she insisted. "I was just . . . surprised. I should have checked the machine. There was nothing—" She paused before starting again. "I'm only sorry about your friend." She felt absurd for a moment, as if standing in a living room with an armload of books were the most unnatural thing in the world. "It's your house," she added then.

"Well, on Sunday I'll be leaving for Providence." He pushed himself away from the phone table and crossed in front of her again. She noticed that the back of his gray T-shirt was black with wetness. "Want some iced tea?" he asked as he headed toward the kitchen.

"No, no thanks." She watched him disappear into the dark kitchen. The light of the refrigerator popped on, throwing shadows across the three white cabinets she could see from where she stood.

"I've put all my stuff in my own room," he called out to her. "You won't even know I'm here."

Lisa nodded her head pensively and moved toward the couch. She put her books down on the coffee table, but then picked them up again, taking them with her up the stairs to the master bedroom and closing the door behind her.

That night she woke up at two-fifteen. The room was stifling. The rumpled bedsheet beneath her body was damp. Over by the windows, the curtains hung motionless. They seemed to be shot through with light in a way she hadn't seen before. The sheer lace seemed almost to be glowing. It was the underwater light from the pool, of course. She must have forgotten to turn it off before she went to sleep.

She rose from the bed and only then remembered that Carl was in the house. Carl had turned the light on, she realized; she hadn't even had her swim that night, so it must have been Carl. He had been watching television when she went to bed. She remembered hearing the muffled crowd noises of a baseball game as she had dozed off.

She heard a dull splash then, and the sound of someone releasing pent-up breath. Carl was swimming. At two o'clock in the morning. She stepped over to the window and pulled the curtains aside. Below her, his black figure was moving through that bright rectangle of blue, the silhouetted arms and legs tracing semicircles in the water. The length of his arms and legs amazed her. They seemed to be moving in slow motion.

She stepped back from the window and sat down on the edge of the bed. It was very hot, but she didn't want to put on the air conditioner. She hated air-conditioning.

Crossing her arms at her hips, she grabbed the bottom of her sweaty T-shirt and pulled it up over her head. The air seemed instantly cooler. She wiped the sweat from her breasts with the shirt and then lay back on the sheets. Her breasts felt vaguely tender as she lay there, staring at the ceiling. She dropped the T-shirt onto the floor and crossed her arms over the sore nipples.

Above the faint drone of the filter, she could hear the spatters of water as Carl broke the surface, diving again and again to the bottom of the pool.

She rarely saw Carl over the next two days. She was at the library for most of the day, and he spent the evenings with his friend at the wake. But there was no forgetting that she wasn't alone in the house any more; Carl made his presence known in countless small ways. He moved things—chairs, lamps, the phone—so that she found herself momentarily disoriented whenever she entered a room he had occupied. He was conscientious about keeping his clothes in his own room, but he frequently left glasses and dishes unwashed in the sink, and he helped himself to her groceries without asking. Even the noises the house made seemed different now that Carl was there; the creaking of the floors seemed sharper, less familiar, and she found herself stepping through the house softly even when he was away.

On the third evening, she returned home and found that Carl had used the bathroom off the master bedroom—her bathroom. He had left a wet towel on the toilet seat, and there were tiny swabs of shaving cream dotting the edge of the sink. She was surprised at how furious this made her. After wiping out the sink with the towel, she marched down the hall and threw the towel with all her might into his room. It hit the side of his metal desk with a moist, satisfying thump and then fell silently to the floor.

She lay in her bedroom with the door open all evening, waiting for Carl to return from the wake. She tried to read, but her mind kept going over all of the little discourtesies he had committed since his arrival: the missing nectarines, the noise of the television at night, his flippant manner toward her. Several times she asked herself why she was so angry, but she could never really frame a satisfactory answer. She was angry—that, at least, was clear—and by the time she heard the front door slam, her indignation was still strong. She waited a few minutes for Carl to get settled before she put aside the book and went downstairs.

She smelled the dense, sweet scent of marijuana as she entered the living room. Carl was in his usual chair in front of the television, a thick joint in his hand sending strings of smoke toward the ceiling. He was watching the late news with the sound turned off.

"Hey," he said as she sank into the sofa to his right.

"Hey," she answered, almost inaudibly.

"You want some?" He held the joint out to her without taking his eyes off the television screen.

"No," she said curtly. It occurred to her that she hadn't smoked pot in years.

Carl inhaled briefly on the joint, held the smoke in his lungs for a few seconds, and then released it so that it momentarily formed a cloud around his head. Then, just as Lisa was about to begin, he said, "What a pain."

She felt a release of pressure in her lungs. "What is?" she asked.

"This wake shit. I hardly even knew the woman, but Dan is really upset." Carl tipped the ashes from the joint into a glass ashtray resting on his stomach. "He keeps crying."

Lisa leaned back in the sofa, her opportunity lost for the moment. "That must be hard," she said finally.

"My dad says you're a pretty good mathematician," Carl said then in a louder voice.

She didn't like the fact that this statement gave her a rush of pleasure. "For a woman," she said with all the sarcasm she could muster.

Carl smiled at her. "The old man doesn't fool you, either, I'm glad to see. An old caveman sexist under it all, like all male mathematicians." He took another pull on the joint. "Not that being male guarantees math ability, even for a Whitelaw," he went on. "Witness my recent SAT debacle. Dad was devastated, as you could probably figure. Someone from his own gene pool getting a 520 in math. I think he secretly hopes that I'm actually the milkman's son." He shook his head at the television set. "You know he named me after Gauss, didn't you? Carl Gauss Whitelaw, can you just throw up or what."

She had heard that story in the department, but she hadn't really believed it. It had sounded too much like graduate-student humor. "It could've been worse," she said. "I mean, it could've been Nikolai Lobachevsky Whitelaw."

"Oh, right, you do that shit, that non-Euclidean shit. That's your specialty, right?"

She looked at him, puzzled. "That's right. Why—how did you know?"

Carl smiled coyly through the rising marijuana smoke. "I read the abstract of your paper in the den."

She slapped a cushion with her open hand. "Carl, you little jerk, that's private," she said loudly, rising from the couch. "Damn it." Carl seemed very amused by her anger, which made her angrier. "And you used my bathroom today, too."

"Hey, that was an emergency," he said, holding up his hands comically as if to ward her off. "Dan was here and we were late for the wake. We both had to shower and shave, so I thought we'd save time if we each had our own bathroom."

She felt suddenly, acutely, ridiculous. "Yes," she said inappropriately, because nothing else would come to her lips. It was more Carl's house than hers, after all. What had she been thinking?

"Never again, I promise," Carl said, looking up at her. He held the joint out again. "Sure you don't want some?" Smoke seemed to be rising through his fingers.

"Oh, use the bathroom whenever you like, I don't care," she blurted finally. "I'm sorry I called you a jerk; I'm the jerk."

"Hey," Carl said modestly.

She walked toward the door to the stairs, but stopped before leaving. She had to hold herself back from crying in frustration. "I don't like being laughed at," she said.

Carl was looking away from her, toward a corner of the ceiling. "So who's laughing?" he said, very quietly.

* * *

She came home early from the library the next afternoon, since she knew that Carl would be at the funeral dinner until evening. The air in the house was thick and stale, and the first thing she did after closing the front door behind her was walk through all of the rooms, opening windows. It was sunny and humid, a generic August afternoon. Cicadas rasped loudly from high up in the trees—a sound that always reminded her of the summers of her childhood in Pennsylvania, when the month of August seemed endless and blessedly uneventful. She had always loved that feeling of time stopping, of life deferred until the fall.

She changed into her suit and went out to the pool for a swim. The water was deliciously cold, and she swam a few fast, hard laps before stopping and floating for a while. But swimming in broad daylight had little appeal to her now after her summer of night swims; there was something austere and boring about it; it was good for cooling off, little else. After breast-stroking another couple of laps, she swam to the shallow end of the pool and pulled herself out onto the slate patio.

"Getting flabby," she said aloud as she dried herself off. She was in reasonably good shape, and she still had what her mother would always call "a nice figure," but she had gained five or six pounds since moving into the Whitelaws' house. Too much good living, she told herself. Then, smiling at the figure she must have been presenting to the neighbors, she started jogging around the perimeter of the backyard, bringing her knees up as high as she could on each step.

She and Phil had run together three times a week during the time they had lived together. Every Tuesday, Thursday, and

Saturday morning they would get up at seven and jog through campus down to the lake. There they would do stretching exercises on the grassy banks for a few minutes before starting their real run. She had disliked the actual running, but always enjoyed being out with Phil in the sharply angled morning light, pacing steadily through a shower of spiraling yellow leaves.

They had always talked as they ran, about anything—faculty members, jazz, Swedish literature. Phil had not yet outgrown his undergraduate arrogance, and he loved to hear himself making pronouncements. Sibelius, he would say, was a bombastic musical joke; at least once a month he would insist to her that Robert Musil's *Man Without Qualities* was far greater than anything Joyce had ever written. Despite his pomposity, or maybe because of it, she loved to hear him talk. He did seem to know a lot, and his conversation seemed so easy and fluid ("Mathematicians don't *have* to be articulate in English," he would say to her. "You have a better and much more efficient language to work with"). Whenever he launched into one of his miniature lectures, she would merely run silently beside him, happy to indulge him. Time, she had always told herself, would mellow him. Time was all that was really needed.

Now, having finished three circles around the Whitelaws' backyard, Lisa stopped, out of breath. "Goddamn it," she said to herself. She resolved to get back to hard daily exercise in the fall. Stepping over to the edge of the pool, she dived in and swam another lap. The water seemed, oddly, warmer than before. She got out again, lay flat on the warm slate, and watched the clouds reshaping themslevs slowly as they crossed the sky. "This is ridiculous," she said. "What is *wrong* with me?" She sat up again suddenly and looked back at the dark, wet imprint she had left on the deck. She felt like going out, like doing *something*, but all of her friends were away for the summer. The town was empty. She twisted a clump of her hair in her hands and watched the water seep from between her fingers and dribble into her lap.

After her shower, she gathered up her books again and, nearly running, headed back to the library.

Carl was lying on the couch, watching a Wall Street report on television, when Lisa came back to the house at ten. He was smoking another joint, and she found the smell of it, which was perceptible the moment she walked through the door, strangely comforting.

"I was just about to call the cops and report you as missing," he said to the television screen as she stepped up behind him. "Long day."

"Yours or mine?" she commented. She let her books fall to the table next to him with a slap.

"Yeah, mine, too." He offered the joint to her. "Choose your drug. There's this and there's all kinds of Waspy liquor in the cabinet by the phone, though I see you've discovered that."

"The ouzo and the Maker's Mark I brought with me," she said as she went over to the cabinet, "and I see that *you've* discovered both of them." She poured herself a snifter of the bourbon. Her eye caught the title of a book in the glass case above the telephone: *Japanese Inn* by Oliver Statler. It was a book she owned herself but had never read. "The funeral today?" she asked as she turned and leaned back against the edge of the telephone table.

Carl held the joint up at arm's length, like a torch. "As of three o'clock this afternoon, Mrs. Paula Danford Ellis sleeps with the fishes."

Lisa stopped with the glass halfway to her mouth. "You're kidding," she said.

"What."

"They buried her at sea?"

Carl thought about this, and then waved the joint back and forth. "It's just an expression," he said.

They were silent for a moment. Carl took a long drag on the joint at the very same moment that she sipped her bourbon. A woman on television was saying something about the growth of the money supply.

"It's hot. I'm going in for a swim," Lisa said suddenly. She put her drink down next to the telephone and stalked out of the room.

When she came back downstairs five minutes later, she found Carl already changed and in the pool. He stood chest-deep at the shallow end, watching his hands make tiny circles on the surface. The ripples carried two bobbing leaves away from him, toward the other end of the pool.

She stepped quickly to the edge, jumped up, and pulled her knees tight against her chest. Her lower back hit the surface hard, and she felt the water part and then close again around her head with a blunt wallop that made her ears ring. When she erupted to the surface, the water fizzed around her body like club soda.

"Cannonball," Carl said matter-of-factly from the other end of the pool. His voice sounded hoarse from the marijuana smoke.

She began swimming laps sidestroke. It felt good to stretch her muscles out, and she pumped her arms and legs hard against the resistance of the water. Five strokes took her from one end of the pool to the other. Turning around, she changed sides, so that her back would always be to Carl as she swam.

After a few minutes, she developed a rhythm that made her feel as if she could continue sidestroking indefinitely. The water around her was lukewarm but brilliant with light. Magnified in her underwater ear, the sound of the filter seemed eventually to pulse in time with her strokes.

Her forward hand hit something suddenly. She identified it instantly as Carl's chest. She stopped swimming, treading water for a moment in front of him. "Ha," he said, grinning.

"*Pardon*," she answered, giving the word the French pronunciation. Then she swam around him and continued her laps.

On the next pass, her hand struck his chest again. Again she stopped, excused herself, and swam around him. By the third lap, it had already become a kind of game. She closed her eyes and tried to hit his chest harder each time, changing her hand so that it struck him now as a fist, now as a pointed finger or a cupped palm. On each lap, he would appear at a slightly different distance from the edge, so that she never knew exactly when contact would be made. Once she stubbed her finger against his collarbone, and it hurt, but she kept playing. She felt no fatigue at all, and tried forcibly to overcome her hesitation every time she stretched out her arm to begin a new stroke.

Then, on one lap, her hand struck nothing until she reached the opposite wall. She paused, smiling involuntarily into the blue tiles that ran around the perimeter of the pool, and then pushed off the wall to start another lap. Again her hand hit nothing. She swam three more laps. Carl was no longer there. She stopped swimming at the edge of the deep end and treaded water for a few seconds before pulling herself out of the pool onto the deck.

She saw him lying down in one of the lounge chairs on the lawn, about thirty feet from the pool. She stood there, dripping, and watched him. He seemed to be asleep. His chest rose and fell evenly in the irregular light.

"So that guy Egan took off, I hear." Lisa nearly jumped back. She couldn't tell whether Carl's eyes were open. "Couple months ago, wasn't it?" he continued.

"Five," she said, not moving. "Guess it was the talk of the whole math department for a while."

"Dad did mention it, yeah," Carl said, stretching suddenly and putting his hands behind his head. "I always thought you were too good for Egan anyway," he added after a pause.

Lisa pulled her hair back and twisted the water out of it. "They teach you that in charm school?" she asked.

"The guy was a pretentious goon," he said.

Lisa, still twisting her hair, walked over to his lounge and sat down on the edge of it. She could still see his chest rising and falling as he breathed. She put out one hand and placed it on his chest.

Carl put back his head. "Oh Lord," he said softly, "she's gonna seduce me, she's gonna seduce me."

"Don't be a jerk, Carl, please," she said. She moved her hand slowly over the swell of his pectoral muscles. "We're being quiet with each other now." Her hand traveled through the hollow of his collarbone and up the side of his neck to his ear. She was amazed at how hairless his body was. His skin seemed to be radiating heat into her palm.

Carl took his hands from behind his head and slowly lowered

them to his sides. Watching her face, he placed his left hand tentatively on Lisa's wet thigh. "Carl," she said, "I want you to lie still for a minute. Just for a minute." She brought her other hand up over his arm muscles to his shoulder.

Carl didn't move. He closed his eyes and seemed to relax the tension throughout his body. His arms and legs appeared to sink deeper into the vinyl of the lounge chair, and then his stomach growled—fiercely. Lisa smiled. She kept her hands moving leisurely over his chest and arms. Something in the action was deeply satisfying to her. Not sexual, yet—she felt no subtle loosening within her, and she was careful to keep her hands away from the erection that was pushing against the fabric of Carl's bathing suit—but his flesh felt solid and heavy in her hands, like the leather upholstery on the library sofa. She lifted his arm once to test its weight. This is a body, she said to herself. It was as if she had forgotten what another body was like. As if Phil had taken away that entire part of her physical experience when he left.

"Now," she said carefully, lifting her arms to untie the strap of her bathing suit, "I want you to make love to me."

Carl opened his eyes. His stomach growled again, making him visibly redden. "I'll bet you say that to all your houseguests," he said, but his face was serious.

"Yeah," she said, then leaned forward and kissed him on the lips. "Every one."

Carl rose from his reclining position on the lounge and, taking her shoulders in his hands, eased her to the warm grass below. Goddamn you, Phil, she thought as Carl peeled the bathing suit away from her skin. Goddamn you to hell.

She reached up and pulled Carl's head down against her chest.

*   *   *

After they had made love, they lay quietly on the grass together. Lisa was on her side, examining Carl's body in the dim glow from the pool lights. It was not at all the way she remembered Phil's body. Phil's body was understated, economical. No connection between that and the extravagant bundle of bone and muscle before her. This fact pleased her. It helped her to convince herself that she was not deceiving herself, that she was not pretending to be with Phil again. This was a new episode in her life, she told herself. She had come back to earth again. To the living.

"Maybe you can delay your trip to Rhode Island?" she asked him. Her voice sounded loud after their long silence. She picked a blade of grass out of the lawn and twirled it between her fingers. "Your classes don't start for a couple weeks, do they?"

Carl was staring up at the dark sky. "Week from Thursday." He turned his head and smiled at her. "It could be arranged, I guess. Let me sleep on it."

Lisa sat up. A cricket that had been trilling in the grass a few yards away stopped suddenly. "It's late," she said, and slapped his stomach playfully. "I'm going to bed. You can join me if you want."

"I'll be along," Carl said.

"I enjoyed that," she said after a pause.

"Me, too."

Lisa stood up and brushed the loose grass from her legs. "Good night," she whispered. Then she turned and walked toward the bright lights of the house, crossing the black waterstains that mottled the uneven gray slate.

* * *

Carl was gone by the time she woke the next morning. He had come to her bed about an hour after she had gone in—she remembered that much—but she had fallen so soundly asleep afterward that she hadn't heard him get up again. When she woke she found only one of his sweat socks in bed with her. His room, which she checked immediately, was empty.

She ran downstairs. Taped to the television screen was a note. She quickly peeled it off the glass and read it, pacing around the disordered living room.

The note was scrawled in green ink on the back of a coffee-stained takeout menu: "Am late for the 7:55. Sorry about leaving, but I remembered that cross-country practice starts day after tomorrow. You were so deep asleep that I couldn't bring myself to wake you up. Sorry about the mess, but hope you'll understand. Thanks for EVERYTHING. Maybe when I come home in October we can get together. I'd like that. Love, Carl." At the bottom was a long P.S. "Mom and Dad just called from Brussels. Bad news for you, I guess. They decided against the Loire Valley trip without me and will be flying home tomorrow. Arriving Newark 5:45. They promise to put you up until September in a hotel. The Nassau Inn, I think. Isn't family money wonderful? Seriously, they're very apologetic. I've never heard Dad so sheepish. Enjoy it. And thanks again."

Lisa looked up from the note and stared out the glass doors to the backyard. For a moment, she felt as if something heavy had shifted in her chest, making it hard for her to stand up straight. Sunlight glinted off the surface of the pool outside, almost hurting her eyes.

What did you expect? she asked herself then. What could

you possibly have been thinking? She looked down at the note again and reread the P.S. Five forty-five tomorrow. The White-laws would be returning in a little over thirty hours.

Lisa turned back to the living room, dropped the note on the coffee table, and then set to work. She carried the armchair from in front of the televsion to its original position near the wall. Then she gathered up the various sections of the Sunday *Times*, which Carl had left scattered all over the living room, and piled them up on the kitchen table. When she had finished tidying the living room, she went to the kitchen and took a nectarine out of the aluminum bowl on the bottom shelf of the refrigerator. She sat down at the kitchen table and bit into the hard pulp of the nectarine.

A wave of nausea welled up in her stomach suddenly, but she fought it back. "Foolish," she said aloud. Her classes would start again in just a few weeks. She would start a new semester, just as she had done many times before. Lisa sat still for a few seconds, telling herself this as she listened to the wind shuffling the leaves of the red maples outside the kitchen window.

Lisa took another bite of the nectarine and threw the rest of it into the plastic trashcan under the sink. Then she went upstairs to the master bedroom, slid open the door of the closet, and pulled her suitcase down from among the boxes and spare blankets on the high, flimsy shelf.

How I Learned to Raise
the Dead of Bergen County

I got my job at my Uncle Louie's funeral. Not that I was looking for work at the time. I already had a job as a stock clerk at the A&P after school. But when Mr. Guswald at the funeral home offered me a position, I took it on the spot. Sure, I felt a little funny—it was my uncle's funeral, after all—but somehow I thought that Uncle Louie wouldn't have minded. He always had such trouble finding jobs when he was alive.

It all started with an idea of my mother's. She thought it would be nice to have someone give a little speech at the funeral—just a few words about what her brother was like, what he meant to all of us, and things like that. Naturally, everybody in the family thought this was a wonderful idea, but nobody wanted to actually do the thing. The obvious candidates were out: Uncle Louie's wife had left him years ago, and the last anyone ever heard of their son, Jack, he was down in the Caribbean working as a "cook" on a "fishing boat." The other close relatives all had excuses. Mom pleaded stage fright. Aunt Lana made it known that her vocal cords were much too delicate. And Uncle Vern said that it would take more creativity than he could muster to find something positive to say about his younger brother. So, of course, I was the one who had to do it. I had won the Sophomore Writing Prize at the high school for a five-hundred-word essay called ''The New Jersey Renaissance: Why We Should Be Proud,'' so everybody thought I would be perfect.

Anyway, the funeral was the next day, so I had about twelve hours to work on the speech. I was up half the night trying to come up with something decent to say. It was tough, since Uncle Louie didn't really fit any of the descriptions people normally use at funerals: loving husband, conscientious father, hard worker. But finally, at about two in the morning, I got an idea. It was something I remembered from when I was a kid, when Uncle Louie would come over to the house with all the other aunts and uncles for our big Sunday-afternoon meals. It was always during the long after-dinner hours, when the sun was getting low in the sky and everybody was scattered around the house, washing the dishes or watching football or taking a nap in one of the free bedrooms. Uncle Louie and I would get together in the basement and stage train wrecks with my father's Lionels. We'd set up all sorts of elaborate disasters involving three different trains, a passenger-stuffed depot, two billboards, and a flock of plastic sheep that we could actually move on a vibrating metal plate into the path of oncoming locomotives.

So I started writing about those afternoons, and about how at the time I thought my Uncle Louie was the only adult in existence who understood what was really interesting in life. This got me thinking, and after a few more minutes I realized that there were other things I remembered. The way he smoked his cigarettes right down to the filters. His tradition of singing ''Waltzing Matilda'' every Christmas Eve. How he would call me ''Mark of the Dark, Dark Forest'' even after I had started going to high school. So I wrote those things down, and anything else I could remember. Finally, at about 3:30 A.M., I finished by saying that I would miss him—that we all would miss him—and that I hoped he was interested wherever he was and that he didn't have any regrets.

Next afternoon, I stood at the front of the blue room in Guswald's Funeral Home and gave my eulogy, right next to Uncle Louie's open casket. I'd be lying if I said there wasn't a dry eye in the house, but the speech went over pretty well. People nodded in recognition at just about every sentence, and by the end, my mother, Aunt Lana, and Karen were sniffling steadily into their tissues. Even Uncle Vern seemed moved. When I finished, he winked at me from the first row and held up his thumb.

It was later, after the funeral, that Mr. Guswald offered me the job. We were all standing at the back of the blue room, giving directions to the funeral dinner. Mr. Guswald, dressed in a somber navy-blue suit, came up behind me without a sound. He's a short, roundish man who wears thick half-moon glasses and a tie clip in the shape of an antique Model T. The main thing I had noticed about him was the way he stood at the back of the room during the wake, nervously smoothing the nonexistent hair on the top of his head. "Ahem," he said now, pronouncing the word rather than actually clearing his throat.

"Yes?" I said.

"Young man," he said, speaking down toward the floor in a confidential tone. "I wonder if I might have a brief word with you in my office."

I looked around. My father was busy explaining a tricky turnoff to Mrs. Kosoff, so I knew we wouldn't be leaving any time soon. "All right," I said, feeling a little nervous.

He led me to his office across the hall and closed the door

behind us. "Please have a seat, Mr. Penfold. Or may I call you Mark?"

"Mark is fine, sir," I said, sinking into the dense leather chair across his desk. "Nobody really calls me Mr. Penfold."

Mr. Guswald nodded wisely and sat down at the spotless desk. "Well, then, Mark," he began, "I just wanted to tell you how much I admired the eulogy you gave for your uncle. It was excellent—personal, simple, yet affecting. Just the kind of eulogy, if I may say so, that your uncle—that most people, in fact—would desire for themselves."

"Well, thank you, sir. I worked on it all last night."

"I see," he said. He took a white handkerchief from his breast pocket and dabbed the back of his hands with it. "I hope you'll forgive me for choosing this moment for the question I'm about to ask," he went on, "but I saw you standing alone there, and I thought—"

"Please, please, don't give it another thought," I said, slipping into his oddly formal way of speaking. I thought I had figured it out. He was probably short one pallbearer for the next funeral and wanted me to help out.

Mr. Guswald gave me a grateful smile. "In this line of business," he began, "I occasionally have a need for someone of your talents. I think it important, you see, that a few personal words be said over the deceased, no matter how old he was or how alone. Invariably, the relatives agree, but few can actually be persuaded to write those few words. What I have previously done in such circumstances is interview the relatives and then compose something myself, which is then read at the funeral. Unfortunately, however, I don't really have the time, our high season is approaching, so it seemed—"

"You're asking me to write eulogies," I asked, "for people I don't even know?"

Mr. Guswald, looking uncomfortable, got up from the desk. "Of course, you would be using information provided by the deceased's relatives. You would be giving form to their own, well, inarticulate emotions. I assure you there's nothing low or cynical about what I'm asking you to do. On the contrary."

I looked down at the pile of prayer cards stacked neatly on a corner of his desk. A eulogist, I said to myself, trying out the title.

"You would naturally be paid. Five cents per word. And let me add that I charge my clients nothing extra for this service. It's all included in the funeral package we provide." He put the handkerchief back into his breast pocket before saying: "I like to think of the eulogy as an integral part of the Guswald Funeral Home funeral."

I looked up at Mr. Guswald. Surely this job would have to be better than stocking shelves at the A&P. "I'll do it," I said finally.

"Excellent, I was hoping you would." Rubbing his hands together, he turned and then removed a manila folder from a file cabinet behind his desk. "Here's the file on Louella Schwartzkopf. A ninety-three-year-old widow with no children. There's not much there—just what I could get from her nephew— but I rely on your creativity. Just don't fabricate." He handed me the file. "The funeral is Wednesday, so we'll need your copy by Tuesday at the latest."

I opened the file. Inside was a single sheet of paper with a few scribbled notes: "Born and raised in West Indies (St. Kitt's?); had a pet parrot (Rose) for last ten years of life; Englewood

Retirement Home; husband a mason (d. 1958); remembers the day McKinley was shot."

I turned the sheet over. The other side was empty. "This is it?" I asked.

Mr. Guswald opened a drawer and brought out a couple of typed pages. "You will be using information from the file to tailor this general eulogy," he said, handing me the pages. "Naturally, since we all share the same human condition, et cetera, there are certain things that can and should be said about everyone at his or her death."

I looked down at the first page of the general eulogy. "Deceased's name and dates here," it said in parentheses across the top.

"You can remain as faithful to the model as you like," Mr. Guswald said. "It will depend on how strong a sense of the deceased you are able to extract from the file."

I got up from the chair. "I'll do my best," I said.

Mr. Guswald shook my hand. "Good luck," he said. Then, just as I was turning to leave, he added: "Oh, and don't get too sentimental about that parrot. Her nephew tells me she couldn't stand the sight of it."

"How morbid" was Aunt Lana's reaction. My mother was only a little more sympathetic: "Do you really want to spend so much time thinking about the dead?" My father focused on the practical problems. "There are diseases, Mark," he told me one night at dinner. "Just remember to keep away from the corpses."

The only person who seemed at all enthusiastic about the job was Karen. Karen is my girlfriend. She's tall—about an inch taller than me—and she has a long elegant face and a narrow nose that swings to the right a millimeter or two at the bottom. Her eyes—huge, intense, mustard-colored eyes—can rivet you at twenty paces. She and I have been going out since junior high, and we plan to get married eventually. We've been neighbors all our lives. She is, believe it or not, the girl next door.

Anyway, Karen and I talked about my new job that Saturday night at the Kinsellas', where she was babysitting for their eight-month-old daughter, Tama. We had been planning to go to the Mount Fuji Steakhouse that night, but then the Kinsellas called and that was the end of that. Karen, unfortunately, is crazy about babies. She's the only girl I know who cancels dates so she can babysit.

"At first, when you told me about it at the funeral, I thought it sounded awful," she said. Baby Tama was lying in her lap, moving like a swimmer doing the backstroke, leaving small milky handprints all over the beautiful wool skirt I spent a fortune on for Karen's last birthday. "But it's kind of like bringing these people back to life, isn't it. One last time, for all their relatives and friends."

Actually, I hadn't considered it that way at all. I had just been thinking of it as a job.

"It's a wonderful opportunity," Karen went on. "Bringing life into the world." She lifted Baby Tama to her shoulder. I could see that familiar sly look in her eyes. A danger signal. Karen's maternal hormones somehow kicked in a few years early, and she wants desperately for us to get married and have a baby. "Mark," she began.

"You know, I should get started on this thing," I said quickly. "Why don't I work on it while you give Tama her bath."

Karen sighed. She's used to me avoiding this topic of marrying and having kids. But that doesn't stop her from occasionally trying it out. She has this fantasy, she told me once, of us going to college together as a married couple. We'd live off-campus, taking turns carrying the baby to lectures in a Snuggly with a big Rutgers "R" sewn onto it.

"OK, OK," she said now, getting up from the couch and lifting Tama toward the ceiling. "I can see that Uncle Mark is not in the mood for family talk."

A line of drool swung from Tama's lower lip, broke away, and fell onto Karen's shirt sleeve. "You can work on the kitchen table," Karen said to me, oblivious, as she put Tama back onto her shoulder and headed up the stairs.

I set to work and, an hour later, I had my draft. It was short—it had to be, considering how little information I had—but I hoped it was all right. I've got to admit I stuck pretty close to the model. In some places, I just filled in the blanks: "It is a long way from (deceased's place of birth) to (deceased's place of death)—long in miles, but longer still in time," and so on. The whole thing was 467 words. That was $23.35, assuming that I didn't get paid just for the words I came up with myself. Not bad for an hour's work, I thought.

When Karen came downstairs again after putting Tama to bed, I gave her the draft for an opinion. I sat next to her on the couch as she read it, watching her face. For some reason, I was incredibly nervous. I wanted in the worst way for her to like it.

After a couple of minutes, she lowered the paper to her lap. "Well?" I asked.

She looked at me. "I don't know, Mark. It's not like the one for your uncle."

My body suddenly felt three times heavier. "What do you mean? What's different about it?"

She shrugged. "It sounds, I don't know, not as natural. I can't picture this woman the way I could picture Uncle Louie."

"Well, of course not," I said. "You knew Uncle Louie. You didn't know Louella Schwartzkopf."

She shrugged again, an annoying habit I'd never noticed before. "Neither did you," she said.

"Exactly! That's my point!" I said, too loudly. "If we knew her, the thing would mean a lot more to us. We'd be able to read between the lines."

"You're upset now," she said.

"I'm not upset." I grabbed the paper back from her. "It's just that you're not being objective. Besides, Uncle Louie was a character. I can only do so much with the raw material."

Just then, Tama let out a cry from her crib upstairs. Karen was instantly on her feet. "Excuse me," she said, in a weird, distant way, and disappeared up the stairs.

I sat on the couch, reading over the eulogy again. I could see her point, I guess. But, then, I didn't have any stories to tell about this old lady. Maybe if Mr. Guswald had pressed the nephew for a little more in the way of anecdote . . .

"I'm doing it over," I said to Karen when she came downstairs with Tama. "You're absolutely right and I'm doing it over."

She stopped on the bottom step with a look of mild surprise on her face. "If you think it's really that important," she said, patting the baby on the back.

"Of course it's important," I said. "I mean, this woman's dead, isn't she? I have to get this right." I went over to the hall closet and got my jacket. "Listen, I'm going home now to work on this. I think I know how to do it." I kissed Karen good night over Tama's tiny shoulder. "And sorry I got mad," I whispered. "Let's say we do something nice with this twenty-three dollars. Go out shopping or something. I'll call you."

I'd gathered up my papers and was stepping into the foyer when Karen called out to me. "Mark, damn it," she said. "Come here."

I turned and came back to the staircase. Karen was still standing on the bottom step. Her face seemed flushed. Her eyes were wide open and I could see the tiny mole in the hollow of her collarbone moving as the blood pulsed under it. "Kiss me again," she said.

I stepped forward and slipped my hand between the back of her neck and her hair. With her standing on the step, her face was miles above me. I pulled her head down and we kissed, for a long time—until Tama, caught between us, let out a little annoyed squeal. "We'll make one of our own someday," I said to her then. "I promise. When we're old enough."

She nodded. "We'd better," she said, without smiling. Then she moved her head toward the door. "They'll be home soon."

"Right." I stepped back into the foyer. "And thanks for being honest about the eulogy."

"I'm always honest," said Karen.

I opened the door, letting in the swirling night air.

"Da!" Tama was waving to me as I left.

Louella Schwartzkopf's eulogy was a great success. Her nephew read it aloud at the funeral that Wednesday, in front of a hypnotized audience of old people from the Englewood Retirement Home. After the service, two ladies—Louella's best friends, apparently—gathered around the nephew, patting him on the lapels and praising the speech. "You captured her perfectly," said one of them. "Yes," added the other, "and you were just right on how stubborn she was about Rose. Heaven knows why she ever put up with that awful bird!"

Actually, I had stayed up half the night trying to figure out that exact thing. The parrot, after all, was one of the few concrete things I had to go on. I'd spent hours poring over the notes, trying to imagine what kind of woman would hate her pet bird and yet keep it around for the last ten years of her life. Her Caribbean childhood suggested one or two possibilities, and so did the fact (which I uncovered after some extra research) that the Englewood Home technically didn't allow pets. So I had finally come up with a picture of an independent, tough old lady who enjoyed a struggle—a nursing-home maverick of sorts, with an ironic sense of humor about her own lonely and pretty desolate situation. Naturally, I didn't go out on a limb about any of this in the eulogy. It was more something I could work from—a sense of a real person—something I could use to breathe a little life into Mr. Guswald's formulas.

Apparently it had worked. Everybody in the room looked happy after hearing it, full of that feeling of pained, sweet nostalgia that people are supposed to feel at funerals. "You're just jogging people's memories," Mr. Guswald had told me when I handed in the speech. "You're helping them release those feelings they want to and should release." Now, looking around, I thought that maybe he was right. But, even so, I wasn't satisfied. And it wasn't just because the nephew who read it was inept (I sat in the back of the blue room cringing every time he stumbled over one of my better turns of phrase). I guess I was feeling that, even if other people—people who knew Louella

Schwartzkopf—thought it was good, it wasn't good enough. I had really just filled in a few blanks.

Later, in the back office, Mr. Guswald shook my hand warmly. "Excellent job, Mark. Really first-rate." He took a key from the pocket of his vest, unlocked the middle drawer of his desk, and removed a large business checkbook. "Mrs. Schwartzkopf's nephew asked me to convey his thanks," he said as he wrote out a check for twenty-five dollars. He ripped the check out of the book and handed it to me. "There you go, Mark. And well earned, I might add."

I looked at the check in my hand. My first fee as a professional eulogist.

"I have another job for you," Mr. Guswald said then. He pulled a file out of his cabinet. "A somewhat younger person. A man. But a similar situation—no immediate relatives except for an older sister."

I opened the file he gave me. Inside was a résumé, a photocopy of a death certificate, and a page of handwritten notes barely longer than the one I'd had for Louella Schwartzkopf. I took the sheet of notes from the file and read them through: "August Henson; 58; heart attack. Sold real estate. Ex-girlfriend a professional golfer (will NOT be present). Had a pleasant manner. Once told sister he felt he was 'missing the mystery of life.' "

I slipped the sheet back into the file. August Henson in five hundred words. That was my assignment.

"Mr. Guswald," I said then, "I wonder if I might make a suggestion."

The smile shifted momentarily on his face. "Yes, Mark. Certainly."

"I wonder if we couldn't try to get a picture of the people

I'll be writing about. A couple of pictures even, of them at different times of their lives. And maybe I could interview the relatives myself. It would save you some trouble, and I'd get to know the deceased a little before I started writing."

Mr. Guswald was nodding his head in approval. "I'll call the sister and see what I can arrange."

"Thank you, sir. It's just that, I don't know, I want to be professional about this." I stood up and put the Henson file under my arm. "Oh, and when do you need the text?" I asked.

"By Friday, I'm afraid."

"It's as good as done."

Mr. Guswald looked amused and puzzled as he rose to shake my hand. "I'm sure it is," he said slowly, "I'm sure it is."

By the end of the month, I had quit my job at the supermarket. I was doing three eulogies a week, and after Mr. Guswald bumped my rate to eight cents a word, I realized that I could make more as a writer than as a stock clerk (even though I spent a lot more time on my eulogies than I ever did at the A&P). I'd spend twenty or thirty minutes—sometimes even an hour or more— interviewing any of the deceased's relatives I could get to sit down with me. I'd probe gently at first, trying to establish some basic facts and figures, but then turn subtly to more interesting areas ("But why, do you think, did she want to move out after you installed the wood paneling in her room?"). Some people were amazingly talkative and open, others needed prompting. Sometimes I practically had to suggest their own memories to them.

"You mentioned that she was a swimming instructor," I said to one woman. She had been drawing blanks when I asked her to try to remember things about her recently deceased mother.

"Yeah," the woman said, nodding vaguely. "Water safety."

"Did she ever take you to the beach?"

"Oh yeah, every summer. Atlantic City, Wildwood. We never missed."

"Well, do you remember what she would do at the beach? Did she teach you how to swim? Did she lift you up over the waves as they broke?"

A flash of recognition appeared in the woman's eyes. "Yeah, she did. She'd lift me by my wrists. I remember she'd say, 'Up and over, love, up and over,' and the cold splash would hit my legs. I used to love that, when she did that."

Armed with a couple pages of notes like this, I could go back home and write up the eulogy. I'd spend hours on it. After finishing the first few, I found I could depart pretty drastically from Mr. Guswald's model and still come up with something that worked. I guess I was developing my own techniques. I varied beginnings and endings, and tried to pitch the rhetoric of each eulogy to a level that seemed right for the person I was writing about.

Normally, the eulogy would be read by somebody in the deceased's family. This was helpful, since he or she could read over the text beforehand and correct any little mistakes or oversights I might have made. But when nobody offered to give the eulogy, Pastor Gioseffi would read it at an appropriate point in his funeral service. This had its advantages. Pastor Gioseffi read with a rich Italian accent that gave a nice extra dimension of poignancy to everything he said. On the other hand, he did have an annoying tendency to toss in a few corny religious quotes at the end of each eulogy.

But, basically, the whole process was really interesting to me.

I'd sit alone in the Plaza Diner after a funeral and think, They all had real lives, these people. Even the lonely, forgotten ones. They weren't just frail old geezers who wandered over to the park every day to sit in front of an empty band shell and worry about getting enough roughage. They had done things—built houses, climbed mountains, smashed up cars. All I had to do was dig a little to give it back to them in the form of a eulogy.

Certainly Mr. Guswald was happy with the arrangement. He said that we were already getting some word-of-mouth business—Guswald's had become the funeral home of choice for a couple of the retirement homes in the area, mainly because of the free eulogy policy. Rumor had it that the D'Amici Funeral Home on Main Street, Guswald's major competitor, was thinking of starting their own free eulogy policy. One pallbearer even heard that they had hired someone—a playwright from Piscataway who had once written obituaries for the Philadelphia newspapers.

"I'm not worried in the least," Mr. Guswald said one afternoon as he wrote out a check. "After all, we have the best in the business writing for us."

I took the check from his hand. It was more than it should've been.

"Just my little way of saying thanks," Mr. Guswald said. "It's a rare gift, Mark. I honestly believe you have a calling."

"Great hands, really great," said Fanshawe Hatch, the embalmer. He was finishing up work on Gina Dallapiccola, the subject of my latest assignment, whose pale body lay under a sheet on the portable embalming table in front of us. "And would you look at that chin line? Not a trace of dewlap, can you believe it? And this a seventy-three-year-old woman." Fanshawe shook his shoulder-length brown hair in admiration. "You're beautiful!" he said, so loud that his voice echoed into the corners of the refrigerated vault.

"So," I said to him, gritting my teeth a little as he injected another few cc's of formaldehyde into Mrs. Dallapiccola's stringy neck, "would you say she had an easy life, then? Her nephew says she was pretty rich."

"Rich, poor. Life can do it to you no matter what you got in the bank, am I right?" He threw the used syringe into a plastic pail and then wiped his hands on his apron. Fanshawe was in his early thirties, acne-faced and fat. There was an odd puffed-up look to his entire body, but he was friendly and smart. And he obviously knew his job. "The best newcomer in the business," Mr. Guswald had confided to me one day.

"Come on," I said to Fanshawe now. "I need to know this for the eulogy."

Fanshawe smiled. "I like a man who likes his work," he said. Then he leaned forward and gently shifted Mrs. Dallapiccola's body under the sheet. Her white arm fell over the edge of the table—right toward me. "No, Mark, lad," he continued, gently taking the arm and tucking it back under the sheet, "this old girl has had an easy time of it, I can tell you that. No hard labor, stayed out of the sun, could even afford a facial now and then. The Good Life, know what I mean?" He looked over at me and pulled the hair away from his face with both hammy hands. "Oh, but there is a trace of a fracture. Bad one, along the left collarbone."

"Any idea when it happened?" I asked.

He kneaded the bone in question with his fingers. "Not too long ago. Two, three years. Never healed right, feel that."

"I'll take your word," I said, writing "Collarbone?" in my spiral notebook. "I'll check that out with her sister."

"And ask her about the scar behind her knee, OK? I'm dying to know where that came from myself."

"Will do," I said, making a note of it.

This was an agreement Fanshawe and I had. In exchange for my keeping him company in the vault, he would give me any leads he could turn up in his examination of the body. I'd found him a valuable source of information. Even when Fanshawe wasn't working, though, I'd go down to the vault after school and walk around the place. Just being near their bodies, I felt, helped me to understand these people. It was almost as if they had left behind a slight aura, a tiny buzz that I could tune into to get a better sense of who I was writing about. I'd open up my files, read through whatever I had, and then just watch the faces, trying to connect what I read with the people behind the faces. It worked, too. Sometimes I'd be blocked on somebody— their file just wouldn't add up somehow—and I'd go down to the vault for a while, sit across from them in Fanshawe's molded plastic chair, and in five or ten minutes I'd have it. The core person. The glue that held the facts together.

Of course, all this took time. "Not at the funeral home again, were you?" my mother would ask me every night before dinner, her chin wrinkling in worry. Even Mr. Guswald seemed a little concerned. "You know, Mark, unfortunately I can't offer you any extra payment for this time you're putting in," he said one afternoon. But I assured him quickly that it didn't matter. "I don't expect it, Mr. G," I told him. "I'm in it for more than the money."

And, really, it *was* more than a money-paying job for me. That's what I'd been trying to explain to Karen for the past week or so. She'd also been worried that I was devoting too much time to my work. "You're exhausting yourself," she said one night. We were sitting on the lavender sofa in the living room of Mr. and Mrs. David Jelco. Janna Jelco, fourteen months old, was standing on Karen's thighs, apparently trying to push her head through Karen's collarbone. It was another of our baby-sitting dates. "Just look at your eyes in a mirror," Karen went on. "They're practically vermilion."

"I can't help it," I said, picking up Janna's battery-powered talking bear. "I mean, I work at it and work at it, and still I'm not satisfied."

"Mr. Guswald seems satisfied."

"Oh, he's just happy because the customers are happy," I said. "But I'm after something more, I don't know. I want to really re-create these people." I turned the bear around and hit the play button underneath its little blue vest. "Hi, kids," the talking bear said.

"But what about all the school you've been missing?"

"Oh, school," I said, tossing the bear into a chair across the room. "School can wait." I slipped my socked feet into the warmth under her thighs. "You can't say I've been neglecting *you*, can you?"

She looked down at Janna's blond head. "Hardly," she said, with a little redness coming to her face.

Actually, we'd been seeing a lot of each other lately. I didn't know what it was, but I felt like I couldn't get enough of her. Her body seemed somehow fuller and richer to me, and her skin had the feel of velour, velvet, some texture that your hands couldn't help wanting to touch. Having sex had always been something we did, I don't know, because we'd been together for so long, and because all the other couples we knew were doing it. But now it was different—like drinking whole milk suddenly after years of drinking skim.

"Well, anyway," I went on, "I feel like I've got a responsibility now. Something more important than school."

Karen rolled her eyes. She lifted Janna from her lap and put her down on the floor next to a pile of She-Ra dolls. "But someday you'll have to think about the money," she said, moving over to my side of the couch and wedging herself in. "You can't be making very much this way. On a per-hour basis, I mean."

"A per-hour basis!"

"No, really, Mark. You've got to think about things like that." Her hair smelled—of library paste or something. I found myself getting aroused. "Someday we'll have to support a family on your salary," she said.

I dug my cheek into her scalp. "Money will come somehow," I said, shifting. "But I've got a responsibility to my people."

"Dead people don't have to be fed."

I grabbed the back of her neck with my left hand and squeezed the muscle, hard. "Don't talk about money," I said.

Her shoulders stiffened. "Mark, you're hurting me," she whispered, smiling.

Mr. Roland Ingbader. Mrs. Millicent Pax. Ella and Dorothy Dinkel. They were all dead and gone in one sense, but they lived on in my eulogies. I kept them all in a red cabinet in my bedroom, numbered and alphabetized. At night I would open wide the drawer and look down on them: Amanda Prickett. Mr. Stanislaw Cheers.

"Mark, take it easy on those potatoes, boy," my father would say to me over the dinner table. Something was wrong—won-derfully wrong—with my appetite. Nectarines seemed juicy and sweet, Pepsi sizzled in my mouth, and even my aunt's brisket of beef seemed to burst with flavor. My mother would watch me tuck into a pile of crisp green beans, staring at me with a look of disbelief. "Are you all right?" she'd ask. Yes, yes, I was all right. Couldn't they see what was happening?

"Love handles!" Karen cried out one night as we lay naked together on her bed. Her parents were downstairs watching "St. Elsewhere," but we didn't care. "Skinny Mark Penfold with love handles," she said, grazing the rounded flesh above my hips with her nose. I felt a deep shudder go through my body. "I could bite them," Karen said with her teeth.

And the eulogies kept flowing. Business at the Guswald Funeral Home had increased by nearly 40 percent in three months. Two extra pallbearers had to be hired, and an assistant em-balmer. "Who *are* all these people?" Fanshawe would ask, sweeping his hand over a roomful of shrouded figures. "Even the Big Guy had a day of rest, am I right?"

But this boom, this inflow of raw material, still didn't satisfy me. I wanted to write more eulogies—and different eulogies, not just for old people. So I wrote one for a man I read about in the newspaper, one of the Acapulco cliff divers, who smashed on the rocks when the waves pulled away faster than he thought they would. And I started looking around me, at people who were still alive. I wrote a eulogy about Mr. Chin, the drivers'-ed teacher. I even did a whole series on the people in my chem-istry lab group. I was asking so many questions that every-body—even some old friends—started avoiding me. Not that I cared. They wouldn't have understood anyway. Besides, I didn't need their physical company any more: I had them all in my files—better, richer, less petty versions of themselves. My life was full of people, and getting fuller by the day, with each new eulogy I wrote. I was writing, creating, repopulating the earth.

Then, one afternoon, Mr. Guswald pulled me aside.

"Mark, may I see you in my office for a moment?" He looked strange. I could see muscles moving under the skin of his cheeks.

"Certainly," I said. We had just finished a funeral for Mrs. Ida Bedell. An impassioned old woman fighting for environmental reform. One of my best efforts.

Mr. Guswald led me into his office and closed the door behind us. A heavy middle-aged woman in a black dress was standing in front of his desk. "Mark, this is Mrs. Harriett Dine, the late Mrs. Bedell's niece. Mark Penfold. Let's sit, please."

I shook the woman's hand. She nodded, but her battleship-gray hair seemed not to move on her head. A timid but determined woman, I thought to myself, composing her eulogy in my head.

"Now, Mark," Mr. Guswald began, "Mrs. Dine wanted to see the author of her aunt's eulogy in person. To thank you for your efforts."

I turned to Mrs. Dine and smiled generously. "It was my pleasure, ma'am. Your aunt was a remarkable woman. She must have been an inspiration to you."

"Well . . ." she said hesitantly.

"As a matter of fact, Mark," Mr. Guswald said, "it was that aspect of your portrait of her aunt that Mrs. Dine wished to remark upon."

"Oh," I said, turning back to her. "Yes?"

"Well . . ." Mrs. Dine shifted uncomfortably in her chair. "My aunt *was*, as you say, a remarkable woman, and of course I think you captured that very well." She paused again, looking down at the black purse in her lap.

"Yes," I repeated.

Mrs. Dine took a deep breath. "And yet I can't help thinking that you might have exaggerated, just a little, her . . . activism, did you put it?"

"You're saying that she wasn't interested in environmental issues?" I asked stiffly.

"No, no," said Mrs. Dine. "But, really, that episode with the sycamore in her yard, she was really just trying to stop her neighbor from, well, she had such a nice view of it from her—"

"Mrs. Dine," I interrupted, "are you trying to belittle Ida Bedell's accomplishment in saving that ancient sycamore?"

"What Mark is trying to say," Mr. Guswald said then, very loudly, "is that from one perspective your aunt's actions might have seemed more significant than they perhaps really—"

"No, Mr. Guswald," I broke in again, "perspective has nothing to do with it. That woman had moral courage."

"Excuse me—" Mrs. Dine said.

"Even," I added meaningfully, "if her own relatives couldn't see it."

Mrs. Dine suddenly turned indignant. "I'll thank you not to tell me about my own aunt. I certainly knew her better than you did . . . sonny!"

"What Mark means—"

"I wonder if you *did* know your aunt better than I did. I researched her life. I built her portrait word by word. You and your brothers left her alone in a nursing home for the last five years of her life."

"I beg your pardon!"

"It's your aunt's pardon you should beg," I said, standing up suddenly. Mrs. Dine's mouth was wide open.

"Now, Mark," Mr. Guswald said firmly.

"I've nothing more to say to this woman," I said. I wheeled around on my heel and walked out of the office, slamming the door behind me.

God, I was ecstatic. By the time I reached the parking lot, I could hardly keep from shouting out. "What idiots these people are," I said to myself, laughing giddily. I was thrilled that Mrs. Dine had objected to my work. Her insensitivity seemed to validate everything I was doing, to make her aunt seem that much more real and noble. "They never understood you, Ida," I said aloud.

I jammed my hands into my pockets and started walking fast across the parking lot. Darkness was falling, and I could see the lights of the Plaza Diner across the way flickering on. I was thinking: More, I have to do more.

"Hey, Mark!"

I turned around. Karen was waving to me. She was in her mother's Pontiac.

Feeling another burst of joy in my chest, I ran over to the car.

"Get in," she said, moving over to the passenger seat.

I opened the door and slid into the driver's seat. I kissed her, hard, sliding my tongue through her teeth until it touched the roof of her mouth. "Mmnh," she said, surprised.

I pulled back and turned the key in the ignition. "Let's drive," I said. I put the car into gear and pulled forward suddenly, making the tires squeal against the asphalt.

I turned into traffic. The Pontiac was responsive and fast. I hit the gas harder, and we sped up Lemoine Avenue, past the fake colonial façade of Fort Lee High School. "Let's find some-place alone!" I shouted over the air blasting into the open windows. Karen looked at me and nodded.

I turned off onto the Palisades Interstate Parkway and sped up even more. The Pontiac's engine roared. As I drove, I kept thinking about my cabinet full of files. All of those people. All mine.

I swerved off the highway at the Alpine Lookout. The car screeched as I hit the brakes. It was a lonely place—just a parking lot on top of the Palisades, overlooking the Hudson River. The trees all around us were dark. And there were no other cars.

I turned off the engine. The sudden silence hit around our ears. But we didn't stop to listen to it. We didn't even stop to watch the lights of Yonkers flip on, one by one, across the river.

Karen's blouse was off. She lay back on the front seat, the light dappling the curves of her body. I leaned toward her warmth and reached into her bag for her diaphragm, but she grabbed the blue case from me and slowly lobbed it out the window. "We don't need that any more," she said, "I'm pregnant."

Layover

The announcement came as I was dozing. The Secretary of State, who was apparently moonlighting as a waiter in a Jamaican restaurant, had just refused to give me back my rice pudding. He was holding it spitefully above his head, as a swarm of iridescent hummingbirds with long streamer-tails began swooping down on it, stealing raisins. I was getting furious. That's when the pilot's voice broke in, saying something about snow.

"Snow?" I said, bolting awake.

The man sitting next to me shrugged. Sighing loudly, he reached forward and pulled the inflight magazine from its pouch in front of him. "Damn," he muttered to himself.

I turned and stared out the plane window. Tiny puffs of cloud were passing in a layer beneath us. I could see their shadows moving slowly across the gray surface of the ocean below. "Snow?" I said again, finding it impossible to believe. Admittedly, it was April—certainly not too late for a New England blizzard—but I was returning from a photo assignment in Jamaica, where it had been sunny and ninety-three degrees. And I had just spoken to my husband, Pete, in Boston the night before; he had said nothing about a storm. But now here was the pilot telling us that Logan Airport was closed, that all traffic was being diverted to the New York—area airports. We would be landing at Newark, where we would clear customs and then await a change in the weather in Boston.

The plane banked suddenly, and the oval of sunlight from the window swept past my clenched hands and up over my shoulder. "Damn," I whispered, echoing the man next to me. I wanted desperately to spend this night at home with Pete. The Jamaican assignment had not gone well. The resort hotel I was photographing—only slightly less surreal than the one in my dream—had been truly, and irreparably, ugly. There had been litter and yellowing vegetation everywhere, and my carefully arranged spreads of Jamaican *haute cuisine* had wilted in the hot Caribbean sun before I could even get a meter reading. And now they were telling me that I couldn't go home. Because of snow. The irony was devastating.

The plane steadied again. As if suddenly set loose from somewhere in first class, the flight attendants came charging down the aisles, offering everyone apologies and complimentary cocktails. I ordered a rum-and-Coke and then turned toward the window again. Even the few clouds of a moment ago were gone now. The sky was totally clear. "Ten inches is what they're saying now, ma'am," said a chubby flight steward in answer to somebody's question.

"They're not telling us the truth," said the old woman in the row ahead of me. She was sitting alone, talking straight into the window. "This has got to be a lie."

"Hello, Dad? It's Elise."

"Elise, honey, where are you?"

The man at the pay phone next to mine was shouting, "Reschedule, damn it, reschedule!" I could barely make out what my father was saying to me. I pushed a finger into my free ear and just shouted louder.

"I'm at Newark Airport. Logan is closed indefinitely and they put us down here. It's an incredible mess."

"Geez, honey, that's terrible."

My father paused. I leaned back against the plastic partition and turned to face the busy terminal. "Can you put me up for the night, Dad?" I said finally. "That's the essence of this phone call."

"Oh God, yes, of course, I'm sorry. We'll be up to get you right away. Mayumi's just about to put a roast in the oven."

"The thing is, the airline is putting people up in motels, but the line's a mile long and I thought—"

"Don't even dream of it. How often do we get you to Jersey, anyway? We'll be thrilled to have you."

I shifted the phone from one ear to the other. A tiny Indian girl in a sari was dragging a piece of Gucci hand luggage across the packed floor of the terminal. "You're sure Mayumi won't mind?" I asked.

"What are you, contagious or something? Just be in front of the arrivals building. Give us forty minutes to get up there. We know the way."

"Thanks, Dad," I said. And then: "Dad? Let's make this a nice visit, OK? A truce?"

"A truce? We've been at war? Nobody told me."

"You know what I mean. Let's just not even bring up the subject, OK?"

"Haven't the foggiest idea what you're referring to," my father answered jovially. "Look for us in forty minutes, then. We'll be the ones with bells on. Bye."

"I'll be waiting," I said, and then hung up.

Gathering up my bags and cases of lights, I found a chair near the front of the terminal, just beyond the frenzied mob hanging around the airline counters. Yes, I told myself, arranging the cases around my feet. I had made the right decision. Nothing could be worse than waiting in that line.

It would be the first time I had ever been alone with my father and his second wife, the first time in the almost fifteen years they had been married. Naturally, I had visited them before—every Thanksgiving and sometimes for a weekend during the summer—but always in the company of Pete, and of my brother and sister, and of their spouses and kids. Never alone. Never without several layers of protection.

My father and I. It was a subject that had even got me into a few arguments with Pete. My father always said I held a grudge against him, that my mother, who had barely spoken to him in over a decade, had planted resentment like a tough weed in my heart. Maybe there's truth in that. I was the youngest child, and youngest children, he would say, always side with the mother in divorce. But the fact of the matter is, I was twenty-one when he left my mother. I was in my third year at Duke, and certainly capable of making my own judgments. And when it came to having to decide whom to live with for my last summer "at home," there was never any question in my mind. Even though my mother had sold the house on Alexander Road and moved back to her hometown in Ontario (which I had never seen in my life), I spent it with her.

It was my opinion, to put it bluntly and simply, that my

father was a cad. That word is really the only one that seemed to describe him accurately. It was clear to me at the time of the divorce that he had behaved dishonorably to everyone—to my mother, to us, even to Mayumi. They had met in my father's grocery store in Princeton, where Mayumi, a secretary for a Japanese graphics firm, shopped after work. He had told her that he was in the throes of a divorce—this at a time when my mother still thought she was happily married to him. The affair went on for six months before my mother found out about it. When she confronted him, he told her that he loved Mayumi and that he was going to move in with her. That simple. My mother—and I—had never forgiven him.

That was fifteen years ago. A long time. My brother and sister apparently had no problem getting over it. They would now shuttle between my parents on alternate holidays, not mentioning one to the other, seeming to get along just fine. Mayumi and my brother would trade notes on gardening. My sister, a travel agent, would bring my father brochures and make hotel reservations for him. I seemed to be the only one who saw all of this as a betrayal—not only of my mother, but of the laws of decency or fair play. Even Pete would disagree with me. He liked my father. Whenever we visited, they played long games of Ping-Pong in the basement, trying out tricky spin shots on each other.

So maybe I was foolish even to hesitate about spending the night with them. We actually hadn't argued about my mother in years. And besides, my plane to Boston would be leaving at eight the next morning. It was sixteen hours we were talking about here. We could at least be civil to each other for sixteen hours.

* * *

They pulled up—Mayumi driving—in the Chevy wagon my father had owned for over ten years. "Hey, lady," he said, hopping out of the car, "you look like you could use a ride." He gave me a bear hug and kissed me loudly on the cheek. "This is somebody who just spent a week in Jamaica?" he asked then, holding me at arm's length. "You're pale as cream."

I shrugged. "Who had time for the beach?" I said, recognizing instantly—and with annoyance—my father's characteristic intonation in my own voice.

"You look beautiful," said Mayumi, pulling up the Chevy's hatchback. She pressed her cheek against mine and then started loading in my luggage. "You father is just joking," she added, her Japanese accent still noticeable twenty years after leaving Osaka.

"Elise knows that better than anybody, Mayumi," my father said. He put his arm around her as she tried to push the hatchback down on the last of my cases. "Except maybe you, who have to put up with me every day."

The two of them kissed then, and I felt a vague echo of that shocked disbelief I had felt fifteen years ago. They were still the oddest couple I'd ever seen. My father is tall and, ever since he quit smoking, round, with salt-and-pepper hair and a bulbous nose. Mayumi is a foot shorter, thin and dark and wiry, with a worn sort of prettiness that makes her look like a well-preserved fifty-five rather than the fatigued forty-six she really is. The fact that she is just ten years older than me makes it hard to think of her as my father's wife, or—even harder—as my stepmother.

"You two girls in the front," my father said, shepherding me toward the front of the car. "And let's get home before that roast burns."

We drove down the turnpike, Mayumi barreling along in the fast lane at seventy miles an hour. My father was leaning forward in the back seat, his hand on my headrest for balance. "So how's Pete?" he asked.

"Good," I said, watching my birth state pass by in all its monumental and endearing ugliness. "He's still mad that I have to travel so much, but he's getting better."

"Hey, that was some beautiful Napa Valley spread in last month's *Modern Maturity*, honey. I'm proud of you."

"He show it to all the customers in the store," Mayumi said loudly, covering her smile with one hand to hide her bad tooth.

"They all remember you, Elise. Mrs. Donaldson, Harriet Turnbow. They still ask about you and the other kids."

"Harriet Turnbow," I said with amazement. "She must be ninety by now."

"Ninety-two," my father said. "She shops with her widowed daughter-in-law, who must be seventy herself." He paused momentarily before adding: "They shoplift a loaf of bread and a quart of milk every Wednesday and Saturday."

"No!" I said, twisting in my seat.

My father was nodding. "Like clockwork. But they're so old, I let them do it. All the cashiers know to let them go."

I narrowed my eyes at him. Something told me that he was saying all of this for my benefit. He wanted me to think that he was a good person.

"I think it's sad, that they have to do that," I said, turning straight in my seat again and looking forward out the windshield.

"No," Mayumi said, "they *like* it. They think they are master thieves!"

"It's true," my father said. "They get a charge out of it. They sure don't *have* to do it. Old Harriet's got more money than God."

I looked down at my lap and smiled in spite of myself.

"They probably think I'm some kind of idiot," my father said, leaning back in the seat. "They make a point of walking right by me and saying goodbye. Geez, the humiliation I put up with."

Mayumi made a little snort and then looked over at me. "Tired?" she asked quietly, putting her hand out and squeezing mine on the seat between us.

I realized suddenly that, yes, I was tired, extremely tired. It was inconceivable to me that I had woken at five-thirty that morning in a hotel room in Montego Bay. "Exhausted," I answered.

"Hey, get a little shut-eye, then, if you need it," my father said, leaning forward again. "I'll shut up now. Let me shove over a minute and you can put the seat back." He slid over to the end of the back seat. "Pull the lever down on your right."

I did what he told me and the bucket seat eased back until I was almost flat.

"There, that's luxury, isn't it?" he asked. "Now close your eyes and rest. We'll wake you up when we get home."

I looked up at my father. The seat was so far back that I was practically lying in his lap. I saw the tops of smokestacks passing in the window behind his head.

"Just dream about that beautiful rib roast we've got in the oven at home," he said, looking down at me.

I closed my eyes and—again in spite of myself—promptly and obediently fell asleep.

* * *

My father's arms were under me when I woke. It took me a moment to realize that he was trying to lift me out of the car. "Jesus Christ, Dad," I said, "you'll kill yourself."

He let me go and I sank back into the bucket seat with a whoosh of air. "You used to love it when I carried you into the house," he said with a mock frown.

"Yeah, and I used to weigh sixty pounds, too." I climbed out of the car and stretched. We were in the driveway in front of my father's house, a two-story brick affair in a quiet corner of Princeton. Above the bare maples in the front yard, the sky was turning that twilight shade of indigo that certain photo editors go wild for. "Can you give me a hand with my stuff?" I asked when my father started heading up the walk.

"We've already taken it in," he said, turning and smiling at me. "We think of everything here at Chez Miller." He came back and put his arm around my shoulder, and then the two of us walked together into the house.

Mayumi was in the kitchen, making little noises of concern over the rib roast. "Maybe a little dry," she said, "but not too bad, I think. Charlie, you set the table and we let Elise clean up upstairs. You luggage is in the left-hand bedroom, Elise."

My father looked at me with wide eyes. "We've got our orders," he said. "Snap to it."

When I had finished and come back downstairs, dinner was already on the table. The whole lower floor smelled of beef gravy—a smell I associated with Sunday afternoons at the old house on Alexander Road, when my parents were still together. Since Pete and I rarely touched red meat, it was a smell that had no new associations to water down the old. I inhaled the scent and felt suddenly very calm and thoughtful and sort of pleasantly depressed.

Dinner—which, on top of the roast, included baked yams, stuffed mushrooms, and sesame seaweed (Mayumi's one concession to Japaneseness)—was delicious, despite her insistent apologies. I sat at the Formica-topped table and ate seconds of everything, amazed that this could be their normal evening meal. My father kept refilling my glass with a terrible sweet rosé—"the house wine" he kept calling it, "only a dollar sixty-nine a bottle"—and soon we had polished off the entire carafe. Sometime after dessert, I had the agreeable realization that I was tipsy, very tipsy. They were, too, by the looks of it: Mayumi sat with a closed-mouth smile, watching my father try unsuccessfully to draw a map of Mexico on his napkin. He wanted to show me the location of a new resort—"a budget Acapulco"—that he had read about in the latest *Travel-Holiday* magazine.

I was having a good time, I realized suddenly. It was like a miniature revelation to me, and I felt a little tug of guilt at my throat as I thought of my mother, living with her sister in a little house in Canada, nursing her decades-old wounds. She would be furious with me if she knew, just as she was furious with my brother and sister—for giving in to him, for buying his line. I'm sorry, I told my mother silently, but I'm having a good time.

After dessert, Mayumi and I were in the kitchen wrapping up leftovers when my father appeared with a small Moroccan box covered with geometric designs. "How about a bit of the old after-dinner smoke?" he asked as he lifted the lid. Inside were six fat joints all in a row. "Charlie!" Mayumi snapped, obviously annoyed.

Flabbergasted. I remember thinking at that moment that I

finally knew what the word really felt like. Here was my father—my father!—offering me marijuana. I looked up at him with I don't know what kind of expression on my face. "Are they real?" I asked.

"Finest Hawaiian," he said proudly. "It's Mayumi's, actually. Doctor's orders. It's supposed to help control the nausea from chemotherapy."

I turned to Mayumi. "What?"

"In remission, in remission," she said quickly, patting my shoulder. "Only a little bit in the left breast. They think they get it all, but chemo is standard."

"I'm so sorry, Mayumi," I said, suddenly feeling a vague ache in my own breasts.

"Nothing to be sorry for," she said. "We didn't want to worry you."

"Dr. Weiss says the prognosis is excellent," my father added. "She's responding like a charm. And in the meantime, we've discovered the joy of marijuana."

"Charlie," Mayumi said, shaking her head but barely able to suppress a smile. "You father is hooked now. It's terrible."

"What, hooked? We save it for special occasions, now she doesn't need it any more. That's supposed to be so terrible? Besides, Mayumi is irresistible when she's high."

Mayumi hit him with a dish towel and flushed deep red.

"Shall we adjourn to the living room?" my father said then in his fake British accent.

We sat in a tight group in the living room—my father next to me on the couch, and Mayumi in the Queen Anne chair to our right. To "set the mood," my father had lit some candles on the coffee table and put a tape in the cassette player. We were hearing the James Bond movie theme (the 101 Strings version) when my father leaned forward and lit the joint he had removed from the Moroccan box.

"I can't believe this," I said, to no one in particular. Even before I took a single draw on the joint, I was feeling an overwhelming sense of unreality. Here I was, smoking pot with my father in New Jersey on a Wednesday night when I should've been in Boston eating dinner with my husband. And all because of an alleged snowstorm I had seen no evidence of. "I can't believe this is happening," I said.

"Here," my father said, handing me the lit joint. "Take a puff of that and you'll believe anything."

I inhaled slowly and carefully. The marijuana *was* good; it tasted sweet and smooth—much better than anything Pete and I had ever found in Boston. Locking the smoke in my lungs, I passed the joint to Mayumi, who took it and inhaled with the technique of an old pro.

"That's your trouble, honey," my father said then, releasing smoke with each word. "You hold on to your preconceptions for too long." He took the offered joint from Mayumi's hand and then put his arm around me. "Why shouldn't you be smoking pot with your dear old dad?"

I looked up at him and watched his eyebrows rise as he inhaled deeply. "Well," I said, "for one reason, because it's the same dear old dad who nearly killed me when he found me and Effie Blumenthal smoking—regular cigarettes, mind you—in the rec room one night twenty years ago."

Mayumi snorted. "Yeah, Daddy," she said, leaning forward and knocking on my father's knee, "how you explain that, huh?"

"Ancient history, ladies," he intoned. He knocked the ashes from the joint into a glass ashtray on the side table. "Geez, how you ladies love your ancient history. You should all be taking a course at the university."

I took another long pull. The marijuana was affecting me amazingly fast. Maybe the wine at dinner had something to do with it. I could feel the pleasant dullness packing in around my ears. And my eyes were already focusing on details—the toe of Mayumi's tiny black slipper, the haloes around the candle flames, my father's dimpled hand on his knee.

"I just spent a week in Jamaica," I said suddenly, and very loudly, "in the marijuana capital of the world, and I never touched a drop. A leaf."

"You were on duty," my father said. "Besides, in the safety of your own home is one thing . . ."

"You father very paranoid," Mayumi interrupted, her accent getting stronger. "Whenever he hear a siren outside, he hide the box of joints. In the refrigerator."

This time, I was the one who snorted. Then we were all three of us laughing, giggling ridiculously as the 101 Strings turned to the theme from *Mission Impossible*.

"Hey," my father said a few seconds or a few minutes later. He squeezed my shoulder affectionately. "I promised on the phone I wouldn't bring up your mother, but, seeing as I don't get to see you too often—"

Alarm bells were going off in my head. I could feel the smile disappearing from my face.

"Now, c'mon," he went on, "relax. It's nothing to get you all upset. I'd just like you to tell her something for me."

"I don't want to be a middleman," I said quickly. "You can tell her yourself."

"That's just it, I can't. When I call her on the phone, she hangs up on me. And if I write her, she sends the letters back

142

unopened. She's a crazy woman on this. After fifteen years."

I had to admit that he was right. My mother was a perfectly charming and reasonable woman—except on this one topic, her ex-husband. Any mention of him made her face go instantly hard and icy. Her "Canadian Ice Queen mode," as my sister called it. "What do you want me to say?" I asked.

"Tell her there are some things I want to talk with her about, about Mayumi's and my will. Some little things about you kids · as beneficiaries."

"I'll try," I said.

"And one other thing. About my funeral. I'd like her to be there."

"Oh, Daddy—" I began.

"No, no, it's something I've got to think about. I'm seventy next year, you know. And this thing with Mayumi's had us thinking along these lines."

I glanced over at Mayumi. She was looking down at the candles on the coffee table.

"Tell her we're not her enemies," my father said. "We never *were* her enemies."

The flames from the candle went misty in the corner of my eyes. "I'll tell her that," I said quietly.

My father drew my head to his shoulder. "That's my girl," he whispered to me, pressing his ear down on the top of my head. Then he kissed me on the temple, the way he used to when I was a girl. "Hey," he said, lifting his head. "Where the hell did that joint get to?"

Later, as we were watching a nature show on television about wildebeests, my father pulled himself up from the couch. "Let me see if I can find that draft of the will," he said. "Is it in the den, hon?"

"Upstairs, I think," Mayumi said. "Bedroom closet."

My father climbed the steps, moving more slowly than I liked to see. When he disappeared, I moved over on the couch, closer to Mayumi's chair. "I feel so awful," I said.

She looked concerned. "Too much smoking, maybe?"

"No, no. About Dad, I mean. I don't know, I feel I've been really unfair to him."

Mayumi looked away, back toward the television.

"I feel like he's been right all along," I went on. "I've held a stupid grudge all these years. I mean, it's obvious that he did the right thing. He loves you more than he ever could've loved my mother. It would've been wrong, maybe, for him to have stayed with her."

Mayumi sighed. "You father is a complicated person," she said after a pause, still not looking at me.

It was a strange sentence. I wanted to know what it meant, but I didn't want to ask.

"You father loves me," Mayumi went on suddenly. "He also sees someone else. Another woman." She was facing me now, and her eyes seemed almost to be closed.

"Are you certain?"

She nodded faintly. "He doesn't know I know." She leaned forward then to pick up her glass of water from the coffee table. "He is not so old sometimes as he seem," she said.

"But why do you let him do it?" I asked her. "You let him just get away with it?"

Mayumi took a sip from the glass and placed it back on the coffee table. "There can be worse things," she said. "I am frightened with my breast. He might leave, I say. Like he leave you mother."

I could feel the skin stretched on my face, as if it were pulled too tight over my cheekbones. My father. I looked down at the tiny stub of the marijuana cigarette in the glass ashtray, trying to keep calm.

Then I heard a creaking at the top of the stairs. "It's just written out by hand at this point," my father said, coming down with the will in his hand. "Some of the old furniture from my mother is mainly what we're concerned with."

I got up from the couch and crossed the room. My father and I met at the bottom of the stairs. "What," he said, seeing something in my face. Then I hit him. I slapped him across the face, as if this were some kind of old movie. My hand stung, I slapped him so hard. Then I ran up the stairs into the guest room, closed the door, and locked it.

The rest of the evening passed without another sound from downstairs. As I lay in bed, I kept expecting my father to knock. He would want to talk to me, I thought, to smooth everything over. That was what he did best of all—talk.

But he never came to my door. My father was smarter than that. He knew his daughter too well.

The person who did knock—next morning—was Mayumi, asking me through the door what I wanted for breakfast. "Just coffee, please," I shouted to her, sitting up quickly in bed. My travel alarm clock read six o'clock, and the sky outside the window was just turning milky.

I showered, dressed, and then carried my luggage into the living room, near the front door. When I walked into the kitchen, Mayumi and my father were sitting at the little Formica table, eating bacon and eggs. "Good morning," my father said. "There's plenty of eggs left, and I know you don't eat bacon."

"I'll just have some coffee, thanks."

"Right here," Mayumi said, placing her hand on a steaming mug in front of the chair to her right. "Still hot enough, I think." She was staring at me with a strange look. I realized suddenly that she was angry. I had made her tell my father something that she wasn't ready to tell him.

We sat and finished breakfast in near silence, my father occasionally asking a question about my flight and whether Pete would be able to meet me at Logan. The airport, according to the news report on the kitchen radio, had been open and receiving flights for several hours. Yesterday's storm was already out to sea. "We must be doing something right to have missed that one," my father said limply. Light was now pouring through the window over the sink. It was a beautiful, butter-colored light—the kind I could have used more of in Jamaica.

"Well," my father said finally, rising from the table, "we're bound to hit some traffic on Route 1, so we should probably load up and take off."

The traffic wasn't bad until just outside the airport. There was a long line of cars waiting to get into the parking lots. People were beeping their horns in frustration.

"Why don't you just let me off at the terminal," I said. "This is madness." My voice sounded strange in my ears. I had said practically nothing during the entire ride from Princeton.

Mayumi turned and looked at my father in the back seat. "Let me help you carry the bags in," he said.

We finally reached the entrance to the terminal. "This is fine," I said. I leaned over and hugged Mayumi. "Thanks for having me."

"Please come to visit again," she said. Then, not letting go of my hand: "Really, please do."

I smiled at her and got out of the car. My father was already unloading my cases of lights from the back. "What a load you've gotta drag along with you all the time," he said. I took two of the cases from him. He slammed shut the hatchback and we entered the terminal together.

The swirling crowds of the day before filled the terminal again this morning. The lines at the check-in counters seemed endless. "You can just put those things here," I said when we reached the end of the right line.

He set them carefully on the floor. "Let me just say one thing," he began.

"Dad," I said impatiently. "Whatever it is, I don't want to hear it."

"But I want to tell you." He was speaking in a low whisper, leaning toward me so that no one else on the line would hear. "Mayumi was right, I was seeing someone else. It was just this stupid, casual thing. But what Mayumi didn't know was that I ended it the minute we heard about her breast cancer. I haven't even seen the other woman in almost a year."

"How noble of you," I said. "And now that Mayumi's in remission, I suppose it's hunting season again."

He frowned, and then smiled sadly. "I'm too old for that kind of thing. I'm seventy next January."

I didn't say anything. My father looked around the terminal with his hands in the pockets of his overcoat. It was the old gray herringbone coat he had been wearing for as long as I remembered. He always wore the collar up, so that his hair feathered over it whenever he leaned his head back. "I meant what I said about your mother," he said then. "I want her to be there when 'that evening sun go down.' "

I nodded, though I knew that my mother would never agree to go to his funeral. Why should she?

My father shrugged. "I've done lots of bad things in my day, I know," he said quietly, "but I've always loved you, loved all of you, even your mother. I can at least take credit for that."

"Yeah, yeah," I said, looking down at my muddy suitcase.

"I just hope you all can say the same when you're my age," he said. Then my father, damn him, hugged me hard. His coat was scratchy against my chin. "Our love to Pete," he whispered into my ear.

"Goddamn," I said, frustrated and angry and close to tears.

He held me at arm's length again and looked straight into my face. "You look more and more like your mother every day, you know that? You have her beautiful neck." He hugged me again, and when his lips were near my ear, he whispered: "I'm a stupid old man, Elise. But I'm getting smarter." Then he was gone—out the mechanical doors to the old Chevrolet waiting patiently outside.

On the plane, as the other passengers arranged and rearranged their belongings in the overhead compartments, I sat back in the seat I had occupied the day before, staring at the cover of the same inflight magazine. I had called Pete after checking in, so I knew that he would be waiting for me at Logan when we arrived. It seemed ages since I had left the airport in Montego Bay. My mental images of Jamaica were already taking on the haziness of old memories.

One of the last passengers to board was the old woman in

the row in front of me. We had spoken briefly on the previous day's flight, so she smiled and nodded when she saw me. Her expression was worn and tired, and she seemed nervous.

"How did it go?" I asked her.

"Terrible," she said eagerly, apparently glad to have someone to tell of her ordeal. "They put me up in an awful motel in East Orange. Torn curtains, smelly sheets—awful! And then no one would accept the meal voucher they gave me. I had to pay for my own." She shook her head. "What I wouldn't do for a home-cooked meal from my own kitchen," she said, and then slid into her seat in front of me.

Poor woman, I thought. What could be worse than being miserable and alone in East Orange, New Jersey?

"Twelve inches in Newton," the woman went on, to no one in particular. "That's where I'm from. My daughter-in-law says they got fifteen in Springfield."

Then, turning and peering at me through the space between the seats, she said, "Twelve inches." She narrowed her eyes. "I'll believe it when I see it."

The doors of the plane slammed shut. "Maybe not even then," I said.

The engines revved up noisily. Looking out my window, I suddenly pictured to myself the plane taking off. I imagined my father and Mayumi looking up at me from the tarmac, from a receding landscape of curved highways, chemical dumps, and factories draped in smoke. Their faces were getting smaller and smaller as the plane took me away, carrying me toward that lingering cold up north.

Health

The refrigerator in Ilona's studio contains a bag of carrots, a bottle of Smirnoff vodka (in the freezer compartment), and the manuscript of her Uncle Mike's unpublished book about racehorses. She heard somewhere that the contents of refrigerators can survive even the most destructive fires. That's why she keeps the manuscript in the fridge; it's the most valuable item in her studio, with the possible exception of her own paintings, which are too large to fit into a meat locker, let alone a midget refrigerator. She takes the manuscript out sometimes and reads it, usually in the late afternoons, when her creative juices reach ebb tide. That's when the vodka comes out, too. She drinks it straight, the way her Russian ex-boyfriend taught her, from a tiny blue-tinted shot glass. The carrots she eats for lunch.

Her studio is at the south end of an old wooden warehouse in Hackensack. The place is owned by a former Franciscan friar who inherited it from his mother. He has no business sense, according to Ilona, and is renting her the place for a hundred a month. She told me this one afternoon as she stared through the west windows at a red sun the size of a turkey platter. The east windows look across a field of weeds and cattails to the Hackensack River.

When my car is running, I'll take a ride out there after a day at the lab and pass the unproductive late-afternoon hours with her. Sometimes we make love on her paint-spattered divan. Other times we just sit around and drink vodka and listen to her Talking Heads albums—on Siamese headphones, so we won't disturb Katha, the epileptic pianist in the studio next door. At seven o'clock or so, if her creative juices start racing back like the tide at Mont-Saint-Michel, she gives me a marked-up delivery menu to drop off at Fong's Panda House and kicks me out. If not, we drive—my white Impala following her white Lincoln Continental—back to her house in Englewood Cliffs, where we make elaborate three-course dinners that we linger over until midnight. Then we go to sleep and have monstrous nightmares together.

She inherited the house from her parents, who died three years ago. As the only child, she also got the car and enough money to keep her in paint, paper, and studio space for the rest of her life. Ilona dedicated one of her earliest series of paintings to their memory. I've seen them; a jagged flame motif runs through all of the canvases. She keeps the series in a corner of the studio, covered with a grimy sheet of oilcloth.

She calls herself a "semirepresentational expressionist" or a "mud painter," depending on her mood and the person she's talking to. She adds dirt from the banks of the Hackensack to her pigments, and smears it all on paper or canvas with the heels of her hands. Her fingernails never come entirely clean, so she paints them with blue nail polish. Sometimes I can taste grit in the lettuce she tears for our salads.

She's tall and incredibly thin—her pelvis shows through the skin like a skeleton's—and her nose is a little bulbous and always on the brink of bleeding. She has thick reddish hair that's usually heaped messily on top of her head and held in place with handfuls of bobby pins, which she sheds at every turn the way cats shed fur.

She's got a quiet, slightly hoarse voice that makes her sound as if she's always coming off a cold. But she doesn't get colds, or even sore throats.

Sometimes she does push-ups in her studio. Once, a couple years before she met me, she punched a guy in a bar and dislocated his septum. When he started bleeding, she gave him her jacket to hold against his swelling nostrils. Then she drove him to the emergency room at Englewood Hospital. My kind of girl.

2.

It all started, really, five months before I met Ilona, when my parents decided to leave home. "We'll be flying down in January, after the holidays," my mother told me one evening as she unwrapped a frozen leg of lamb. I remember the meat smoking in her hands like something on fire. "Dad and I think you should stay here as long as you like," she went on. "When you want to move, tell us and we'll tell the realtor to sell. Meantime, you've got the place to yourself."

They were moving to Florida, to a place just outside Jacksonville. My sister, Annette, had moved there three years earlier; Annette and her husband lived in a twelve-room hacienda-style house three hundred yards from the beach. "Florida!" I had nearly shouted when Annette first told me she was going. "I thought only old people moved to Florida."

And now my parents—old people—were following her south. For their health, they said. My father was diabetic and my mother had had two mild heart attacks. "The warm winters will be better for your mother's heart," my father told me that evening, after we finished the leg of lamb. He was staring down at his thick, hairy hands as he spoke. He knew it was going to be difficult for me.

When January came, I took the afternoon off from the lab and drove them to the airport. On the way to the gate, we had to stop while my father tied his shoe. He did it slowly, carefully, almost as if he had to try hard to remember how to do it. My mother, meanwhile, smiled sadly and asked me whether I thought the girl behind the pretzel cart looked a little bit like Annette. "A bit," I said, though the girl must have been at least ten years younger than my sister.

Then they were gone, and I was alone in the eight-room split-level house that I had grown up in. I would come in at night and the lights would all be out. I could move the furniture around in the living room and nobody but me would know.

"Empty-nest syndrome," I would joke to my friend Joyce at the lab. Maybe it really was. I found myself working later and later most evenings, clearing up unimportant paperwork at the lab until ten or eleven o'clock. Other nights I'd go home and drink rum-and-Cokes. I'd sit in front of the TV and watch reruns of situation comedies deep into the night. Ha-ha, I'd say aloud at the screen, a few seconds after the canned laughter stopped.

Once, on a rainy Saturday night, I drank through an entire bottle of rum. At midnight, with the blue light of the television flickering around the walls, I climbed the three groaning, un-carpeted steps to my parents' old bedroom. I stepped up to the bed, turned back the ratty brown spread they had left on it, and looked at their pillows. They were flat, uncreased. I picked them up and crushed them to my face—first my father's, then my mother's. It was something I had done as a kid, when I was alone in the house, scared or lonely or just bored. Now, as then, the pillows held their scents, even though my parents hadn't slept on them for weeks. My father's smelled of sweat, camphor, and wintergreen (from the Ben-Gay he used on his forever-aching neck muscles); my mother's smelled of soap.

I inhaled deeply, letting the dusty aromas loosen the tightness that had wrapped itself around my shoulders. Downstairs, the voices on the television went on—murmurs addressed to an empty room.

The next morning—a bright, innocuous Sunday morning—I telephoned my parents. "Go ahead and call the realtor," I told my mother. "I think it's time for me to leave."

3.

I met Ilona that spring—at a pinochle game—on the night before my mother's bypass operation. By then I was living in my new place: a three-room basement apartment in a big brick house on a flat-topped hill. The house was surrounded by rhododendrons and dogwoods and begonias. From the end of the gravel driveway, I could see the roof of the old house, three blocks away.

My father had called in the afternoon. The special diet my mother was on, he said, was not really helping her; the cardiologist thought she might be in danger of another attack. "They say it's not an emergency, but that the sooner it gets done, the better. I'll tell you if you need to come down." The operation was slated for the next morning, not (he quickly assured me) because it was rush-rush, but because someone had died before surgery and opened up a slot in the schedule. "The procedure's pretty routine, they tell us," my father said.

"And Dr. Tucci says this bypass should—I repeat, *should*—do the trick for her."

John Peebles, an acquaintance from Rutgers, had called about ten minutes later, just as my father's news was beginning to penetrate the layer of numbness that seemed to surround my body. John's usual fourth for pinochle was sick with the flu; could I maybe fill in? I remembered the red bumper sticker that hung over John's bed in his dorm room at school—PINOCHLE OBLITERATES THOUGHT, in black Gothic lettering. "I'll bring a six-pack of Bud," I found myself saying into the phone. "But you'll have to pick me up. My car's in the shop."

Ilona was one of the other players. John introduced her as "Ilona Lee, *artiste* from Tennessee," though she had no discernible accent. Her fingers were stained black around her blue fingernails, and she threw down her trump cards the way medieval knights must have thrown down their gauntlets. She talked steadily through the game—about treacherous gallery owners, deadbeat clients, and a newspaper critic in Philadelphia who had called her work "tedious and primitive." Then, in the middle of a hand, she said something about her "parents' demise."

I felt a slight tightening of the muscles in my legs when she said this. Do parents have demises? I wondered. Was this the way you talked about your parents' death when they were gone? I looked over at Ilona and tried to imagine what type of person would use an expression like "my parents' demise." "Your play," she said then, lifting her eyes to mine.

When the game broke up, I asked Ilona for a ride home. I guess I wanted to hear more about her parents, and, besides, she was going more or less in my direction anyway. Eastward. She lived in Englewood Cliffs.

We sat side by side in the front seat of her white Lincoln. At first we talked about the obvious things—my lab job, the other pinochle players, her studio—but our voices seemed absurdly small in the enormous, vinyl-smelling space of the car. There were long silences between our sentences. I watched the empty lanes of Route 80 speed past the windows, dreading the moment when I would have to get out of this car and enter my lightless basement. I knew that, once I was alone in my own apartment, I wouldn't be able to stop myself from thinking about my mother in some high, white hospital bed, breathing faintly and wearing one of those plastic identification bracelets around her narrow wrist.

We had been silent for a few minutes when we passed the first sign announcing the exit for Fort Lee. That was when I asked about her parents' demise.

She seemed surprised that I asked. "With most people I meet, that's probably the last thing they want to talk about," she said. "Sometimes I think they sit across from me and dread that I'll bring the subject up. You must be some kind of ghoul or something, eh?"

I told her about my own parents—that they were both very sick, that they had moved to a place a thousand miles away from me, that my mother was having open-heart surgery in eight hours.

"Oh," she said. "Sorry." She stared hard at the road for a few seconds. Then, finally: "My parents were killed in a fire, in a hotel in Lisbon a couple of years ago, two days before my twenty-sixth birthday."

When I didn't answer, she turned to look at me and then went on. "It's fine, it's over now. I survived. This is their car, in fact. I inherited it. The house, too, and gobs of money. I still live in the house, but I spend most of my time in my studio.

Painting is what I do now, all day and all night. I'm painting till I drop dead, hopefully at age ninety-three." She let out a little mirthless laugh then, like a period at the end of her sentence.

"How did you feel," I asked her, "when it happened? When you first heard about it?"

She shot me a worried sidelong glance. Then she answered: "Look, Roscoe, it doesn't pay to go into those things over and over again. Believe me, I know."

"Sorry," I said, looking away and out the window again.

"Your mother will be fine, don't worry." Ilona sped up and changed lanes. We sat quietly as the gargantuan Lincoln ate up another mile of dark, empty highway.

"Hey," she said then, keeping her eyes on the road. "You want to come home with me?"

It took me a moment to realize that she was serious. "Is that just to make me feel better?" I asked.

"I got the idea when you got into the car. It was supposed to make me feel better. If it's making you feel better, too, so much the better, no?"

I hesitated before answering. "Can you drive me home by nine in the morning?" I asked.

"If she's going in at nine, they won't have any news to report until at least ten, but I'm driving you home by six if you want me to."

"Nine is fine," I said, wondering what my father would say if he knew I was spending this operation eve away from home. "I'll make pancakes in the morning if you want. I make good pancakes."

"I don't eat breakfast," she said, and those were the last words we spoke until we reached her house in Englewood Cliffs.

* * *

"Please don't tell me how nice the place is," Ilona said as she swept through the lavish, carpeted living room, turning on lights. "I had nothing to do with making it that way." She had said this before, I could tell—to other guests; it was another line like "my parents' demise."

I stepped down into the sunken living room and wandered among the maroon leather chairs, white marble tables, and black ceramic lamps. The place looked like something out of the magazines that Annette, with a certain amount of irony, fanned across her sideboards in the Jacksonville hacienda. Except that there were a few subtle dissonances. The gladiolas in the shiny black vase in the corner were dead and brittle; a glass bowl on the coffee table held a pair of lavender Betty Boop earmuffs.

While Ilona lit the gas-fed log in the fireplace and opened a bottle of wine, I stood in front of an illuminated oil painting of a man in a gray suit. "This your father?" I asked.

"God, no. My father always wished he looked that good. That's my Uncle Mike, Mom's brother. Dearest man in the world, though a bit on the old-fogey side. Here," she said, handing me a knife-thin, tuliped glass of wine. "White Zinfandel. Cheapest drinkable stuff in the store." Then she took off her noisy clogs and tucked her feet beneath her on the sofa.

"You grew up in this house?" I asked, settling on the sofa next to her.

"From age six on. We lived in Knoxville before that."

My wineglass tapped as I placed it on the marble coffee table.

"The money comes from my mother's side, if you're wondering," she went on. "Generations upon generations of lawyers. Beauregard is their name, can you believe it? Uncle Mike's got his own firm in Knoxville, when he's not out at his horse farm, that is. And see that mantel clock? Belonged to Andrew Carter Beauregard, attorney to the Confederate States."

"And this is how it looked when they lived here?" I asked.

"Oh, I've moved a few things. And the bedroom's entirely different. But I'm in the studio morning to night, so who needs to redecorate?"

I thought of the house I grew up in. It was now occupied by a Greek family who had repainted it a robin's-egg blue.

"So what about your family?" she asked. "What kind of a name is Boghosian anyway?"

"Armenian," I said. "Both my parents were born there."

"Armenian," she said, a little puzzled.

"You know. We're the ones who are just like Jews, only nobody knows about our holocaust. The Turks don't even acknowledge that it happened."

Ilona shifted her weight on the sofa. "Ever think of visiting there yourself?" she asked.

"I did, three summers ago. I even started writing a travel article about it, but it turned into a long treatise on the 1915 massacres. My father read it and said he was proud of me for not forgetting my heritage. He wants me to turn it into a book, which I've actually considered doing."

"You should, you should," she said, being polite.

"I don't really have the energy for that kind of thing after a day of pithing frogs and making tissue cultures. Besides, I'd just be doing it for my parents' sake, and the way things are going," I said, thinking again of that plastic ID bracelet around my mother's wrist, "they'd probably be gone before I could ever get it done."

Ilona frowned and put down her wineglass. "You're a real depressing guy, Roscoe. This little tryst of ours was supposed to make us feel better."

"Oh, right," I said, staring into the crackle-less fire. "Party, party, party."

She leaned forward then and kissed me once on each eye.

We made love slowly, awkwardly, through a fine haze of fatigue and White Zinfandel. As we lay on the king-size bed in the master bedroom, I tried to forget that this was not really Ilona's bedroom—at least it hadn't been until three years ago. The sheets smelled vaguely of men's cologne. Her father's?

When we had finished and lain together for a few minutes, Ilona sat up and popped her contact lenses into her cupped hand. "I feel better," she said as she snapped shut the lens case and turned out the lamp. "Do you?"

"I think I do," I said.

I turned away and she folded herself against the contour of my back, wrapping her arm around my solar plexus. "I'm glad," she said, her voice on my neck.

I lay with my eyes open until the objects in the bedroom became visible in the dim moonlight from the windows. Ilona's breathing was becoming regular against my back. "Ilona?" I whispered.

It took her a moment to realize that I had spoken. "I was asleep," she said.

"I usually can't fall asleep without the radio. Do you mind if I turn it on?"

"Anything you want," she said.

I reached over and adjusted the clock radio until I found WINS, the all-news station.

"This is what you sleep to?" she asked after a moment.

"The stories start to repeat after twenty minutes or so. The monotony lulls me." I wedged myself harder against her and yawned. "Good night."

"Yes," she said. She heaved a big sigh, ruffling the hair at the back of my head with her breath. Then she lay still, pretending to be asleep, but her breathing didn't become deep and regular for over a half-hour—not until after the four o'clock news roundup, the weather bulletin, and a short, despondent plea to take charge of life and attend a school for tractor-trailer drivers.

When my eyes opened the next morning, I found myself staring directly at the digital readout on the clock radio. I was just in time to see it flip from 9:09 to 9:10. By the time it flipped to 9:11, I was already buttoning my shirt and repeating Ilona's name over and over again, louder each time.

"No breakfast," she muttered from the depths of the pillows.

"It's nine-fifteen; I'm missing my call." This didn't seem to register with her. "I need a ride," I said, my voice involuntarily harsh.

"Oh, goddamn, I'm sorry," she said. She whipped back the bedsheets and landed her feet into a pair of silk, Persian-looking slippers. "I'm usually awake before seven no matter how late I go to bed."

Ten minutes later, we were pulling up in front of the house in Fort Lee. Ilona looked disheveled and bleary-eyed in her bathrobe and glasses. I kissed her quickly and said, "I'll call you," but I had slammed the car door and was already halfway to the basement door before I realized that I didn't have her number.

There was no answer at either my parents' or my sister's in Jacksonville. I let the phone ring twenty times at each place before telling myself aloud that of course they were all at the hospital, where I should have been with them.

I looked at my watch. 9:37. Nothing terrible could possibly have happened in thirty-seven minutes, could it?

I made myself a cup of coffee and sat down next to the phone by the window. Mrs. Bromberg and Mr. Yamada—my unmarried, middle-aged landlords—were flitting around the backyard, billing and cooing over the rhododendrons. Mr. Yamada had been the previous occupant of my basement apartment, living in Fort Lee for a three-year stint with the American branch of a Japanese tire company. At the end of the three years, he had got himself an indefinite extension and moved upstairs with Mrs. Bromberg, a widow with political connections. Now, watching them together in the backyard, I suddenly wished that I had invited Ilona in to wait with me. I knew that it would have been unfair of me to ask her—we had only known each other for fifteen hours, after all—but I felt she would have come in anyway. I imagined her at the stove in my little closet kitchenette, pouring water into a cone of ground coffee.

I looked at my watch again. It was getting late. "God, God, God," I said aloud. Outside, Mrs. Bromberg cackled from behind the rhododendrons.

The phone rang at 11:45. I ran toward it and grabbed the receiver, barely capable of saying hello before I had heard my father's small voice saying, "She's fine, Roscoe. The doctor says she's doing just fine."

* * *

I was swabbing up the last of my breakfast—nitrates and cho-
lesterol, as my mother called bacon and eggs—when Ilona's
call came through about an hour later. "Everything OK?"

"My mother's fine," I told her, feeling expansive and relaxed.
"How did you get my number?"

"Do you mean, how did I distinguish you from all of the
other Roscoe Boghosians in the book?"

"Oh, right," I said, smiling. Outside, framed in the window,
Mr. Yamada was holding up a long-rooted dandelion for Mrs.
Bromberg's inspection. As she stooped to get a closer look, Mr.
Yamada quickly slipped the dandelion down the front of her
shirt, causing Mrs. Bromberg to shriek with delight. "This is
really nice of you to call," I said.

"Yeah, it is. Listen, how'd you like to drive with me to my
studio and see the work?" "The work" is how Ilona refers to
her paintings. As if they're already a part of our collective cultural heritage.

"I can be ready by one-thirty," I said.

She picked me up in the Lincoln. Ilona looked freshly scrubbed
in the spring sunshine. She wore a bright-red sweatshirt (which
clashed with her reddish hair), horn-rimmed sunglasses, paint-
smeared jeans, and tennis shoes. "The studio's just the other
side of the Hackensack," she said as we accelerated into traffic
on Route 4. "When the work's going shittily, I call it the River
Styx, yuk-yuk."

Her studio was exactly what I had imagined: an enormous,
cluttered white room with twelve-foot ceilings and windows on
three walls radiating brightness. The floor, covered with narrow

sneaker-prints and dirt scuffs, was littered with paintings in various stages of completion. Folded pieces of paper were being glued to other pieces of paper and held in place by piles of jacketless hardcover books. I picked up one of the books—*The Life Beyond: Do We Die at Death*?

"I buy them by the pound," she said, taking the book from me and placing it back where it was. Then she led me across the room to the one windowless wall. "These are a couple of finished ones." Five six-foot-square, ragged-edged canvases hung there—all shiny browns and blacks, laced with raised stitch-marks and painted hieroglyphs. Little red arrows pointed meaningfully toward smears of black mud. Pieces of frayed rope hung from laminated screws and bolts stuck through the canvas.

"I love them," I told her. And I did, instantly; they were stark and somber, and the hieroglyphs seemed like symbols that had nothing in particular to symbolize, but that created an aura of withheld secrets.

"They're part of a sequence called *Animal Magnetism*," she explained. "I'm showing them at a gallery in Philadelphia in July. When everybody's away at the beach."

We spent a couple of hours in the studio, drinking black coffee and looking at her other series, including *Consuming Fire*, the one dedicated to her parents. Then (prompted by a collection of Kafka's stories holding down the edge of one of her paintings) we got into a conversation about what insects we would choose to be if we were forced to be insects. Ilona said she would choose to be a cockroach, but a rural as opposed to an urban cockroach, since people in the country didn't step on bugs the way they do in other places. I said I would be a praying mantis.

Later on, we lay together on her divan. I was watching the shadows of her canvases, trying to perceive their slow movement across the floor as the sun dipped lower and lower in the windows. Ilona was asleep beside me, snoring in a quiet, charming way. I could feel her chest rise and fall under my hand—like a respirator bag, inflating, deflating, and then, with the infallibility of a machine, inflating again.

4.

Joyce was filling the food trays with treated pellets. "Tennessee, huh?" she said, shepherding the pellets into a pile with gloved fingers. "Got to watch out for the Southern-belle types, you know. They've got their secret priorities. She'll have you registered at Saks before you even know it."

I took a tray from her table and brought it over to one of the cages. "Not this Southern belle," I said. The mice were making the desperate squeaking sounds they always made at feeding time. I opened the slot and slid the tray in quickly. "Ilona's not the registering type."

"Oh, you'd be surprised." Joyce, the other senior assistant in the Secaucus lab, was also one of my best friends. She was around fifty years old, with a tough, wizened face and wrinkled, bony hands inside her rubber gloves. She had been divorced twice and dumped, she said, more times than she cared to think about. Joyce had a snide remark for every would-be romance she heard about, but once I caught her in her cubicle at lunch hour crying over the last few pages of *Jane Eyre*.

"She's a bohemian *artiste*, my dear Ms. Winchester," I said. "One with a white Lincoln Continental, granted, but a bohemian *artiste* nonetheless."

"Oh, one of *those*," she said, putting down the bag of pellets and picking up the last dish. "Lives only for her art, right? I had a

1 6 5

husband like that once. Transformed all of his emotions into long, incomprehensible poems and didn't have any left over for me."

I laughed, but the image of Ilona's *Consuming Fire* paintings flashed uneasily through my head. "If I had a nickel for every one of your alleged husbands," I began, but just then the phone in my cubicle let out an electronic warble.

"Hello, Roscoe?" I immediately recognized Ilona's voice over the phone. It was a Tuesday, two and a half weeks after we had first met. We had seen each other five or six times since the afternoon at her studio—once to go bowling and a couple of evenings to go out to eat—and I had spent the night at her house each time. "Listen, sorry to be calling you at work, but think you can drive out to the studio tonight after you get off? There's somebody here I want you to meet."

"Sure, I'd love to," I said. "Who is it?"

"It's a surprise. Can you make it by seven? Your car's fixed, isn't it?"

"Picked it up this morning," I said. But I was thinking: Why does it have to be a surprise?

"And could you stop at Fong's on the way in? I'm leaving them an order this afternoon. Just ask for the one under the name of Beauregard."

"Beauregard?" I asked, trying to remember where I had heard the name before.

"Beauregard," she said.

"I'd like you to meet my beau, Roscoe Boghosian," Ilona twanged, hanging on the arm of a tall, middle-aged man with reddish-blond hair and a gray tie with a tight, out-jutting knot. "This is Michael Davis Beauregard."

"Uncle Mike is what she means." The man, laughing as he spoke, reached out his hand. "And I don't talk anything like the way she makes fun of," he said, talking exactly the way she had made fun of. "Pleased to see you there, Roscoe."

"And you, sir," I said, finally making the connection between this face and the one in Ilona's oil portrait.

"Mike had to see a client in the city, so he stopped by on his way back to Newark Airport." Ilona grabbed my hand and pulled the two of us to the far corner of the studio, where she had set up a spindle-legged card table with three chairs. "So far, I've gotten him to take off his jacket. If we're lucky, we might even get him to loosen up that awful tie. Is that the order from Fong's?" she asked me.

I held up the paper bag in my other hand.

"Oh yes, I recognize the grease stain." Ilona sat us down in the chairs and ran toward the little refrigerator. "Mike's flight is leaving in three hours, so we don't have much time," she said breathlessly. "He's got to be back in Knoxville before Grandma Beauregard's curfew."

"I wanted to take you both someplace nice," Mike said to me, looking a little embarrassed. "But Ilona forbade it."

"Oh, he would have taken us to some stiff Italian place with a maître d'," Ilona said with a huff. She put down three glasses and a vodka bottle veined with frost. "The waiter would have said things like, 'And what would the lady desire?' Yuk."

Uncle Mike looked at me with a helpless expression and shrugged. "I like Italian food," he said.

Ilona let out another huff.

"Ilona's been promising to read me some of your book on horses," I told Mike as Ilona poured the vodka.

"Good God, do *you* have a copy of that, too?"

167

"I do," Ilona said. "Mom gave it to me years ago."

"Ilona says it's wonderful. Very personal."

"Tell the Durham publishers that," Mike said with a grimace. "They called it 'unprofessional.' "

"Durham," Ilona said, disgusted. "Durham has about as much appreciation for idiosyncrasy as I do for designer running shoes."

"We both were rejected by Duke University," Mike confided.

"Yes, *quelle tragédie*." Ilona's eyebrow went up. "Wait," she said then, patting Mike's shoulder, "remember this? 'I've just been down in Chapel Hill, my dear, shooting peasants.' "

Mike smiled and gave what was apparently his line: "No, no, my dear, you mean shooting pheasants. You don't know your game birds."

"No, no, my dear, I mean shooting peasants. You don't know Chapel Hill."

Then the two of them cackled together in perfect unison. I sat across from them and shook my head.

"Anyway, Ilona," Mike said when they were finished. "I really want that manuscript back. I've made an oath to destroy every surviving copy of it."

"Ha!" Ilona said. She lifted her glass. "To the author of *Horses I Have Known*."

"No, no," Mike said, "to the eventual disappearance of all known copies of that embarrassment of my youth."

Ilona narrowed her eyes. "Over my dead body," she said, and then she knocked back the vodka in one quick move.

Later, as we drove to her house after dropping Mike at the airport, Ilona was quiet. She had insisted on driving herself, since her "two men," as she now called us, hadn't held their alcohol as they should have. Mike protested, but capitulated in the end. "There's no opposing this one, you know, Roscoe," he told me as the three of us piled into the front seat of the Lincoln. "Consider yourself warned." Now, after seeing him off on the last flight to Knoxville, we were barreling north along the turnpike, wrapped in a contented alcoholic fog—or at least one of us was. When Ilona said something about returning Mike's rental car to the airport next day, I realized that, while I was floating, she had been thinking, concentrating, planning. It made me feel absurdly safe.

"You know, Roscoe," she began, after a long silence during which I had almost fallen asleep against the upholstered door, "where I come from, this night marks an important point in a young man's courtship. You've met my family."

I opened my eyes and saw her smiling at the highway as a sheet of light swept past her face. "Not bad for two and a half weeks. Most Knoxville boys don't reach this point for months."

"Mike's great," I said. Then, after a moment: "I only wish I could've met your parents."

Ilona kept her eyes on the road. Another sheet of light started creeping up toward her neck.

"Was your mother anything like Mike?" I asked.

Ilona turned to check her blind spot and then changed lanes. "No," she said at last, "not really," and I understood that the conversation had ended.

5.

Ilona was axing boyfriends, she informed me one day. None of them had been serious, but a few had been regular dates. She said that men were like comets, each with his own periodicity:

some of them called once every two weeks, others once a month; one guy, she told me, called her once a year—on the Fourth of July, to go to see the fireworks at Overpeck Park. But now, as each one checked in on schedule, she was telling them thanks but no thanks: she was seeing someone seriously.

Meanwhile, we were spending enormous chunks of time in her studio. I would read to her from *The Life Beyond—Do We Die at Death*?: "I was in this dark tunnel, and there was this buzzing noise, like hundreds of bees all at once, and I was following this distant pinpoint of light. . . ."

One Saturday, as we were moving a couch in her living room at home, she asked to see my article on the Armenian massacres. "It seems important to you, so I should know about it, no?" I gave her my only copy and then didn't hear about it again for several weeks. I was just beginning to think that she had lost it when, one afternoon in July, I drove out to her studio and found a bunch of new paintings, all slashed paper and red pigments. "This some new series?" I asked her.

"It's called *Armenia*. I'm using your article as a reference. Mind?"

"My father will fall in love with you," I said.

It was because things seemed to be going so well that I was surprised—shocked even—when she refused to see me one night. "I can't, Roscoe," she said over the phone. "I really can't."

"But we said tonight we'd get together."

"It can't be tonight, I'm sorry."

"Just for ten minutes, then. We can time it on the clock. Where are you, at the pay phone?"

"Damn it, Roscoe. What the fuck do I have to do? Do I have to hang up?"

"Five minutes! I don't understand. What's wrong?"

"Just let me alone for a while, OK? I don't want to talk any more now. I'll call you. Goodbye." I heard a click and then that blanket of muffled silence: Ilona had hung up.

I sat at the phone table for a long time, staring at my living room. The light was failing, making little pools of murkiness in corners and under tables and chairs. Twilight. It was the time of day when people looked up half-consciously from what they were doing to flip on a lamp, when smells of cooking reached them from another room, where other people—mothers, spouses—stood at warm stoves and prepared dinner, raising their voices to make themselves heard over the sizzle of whole-some potatoes frying in a pan.

Ilona had reclaimed that time of day for me. Before, I had hated early evening. It was when I'd get those calls from Florida— my parents' voices speaking of things like arrhythmias, choles-terol, and kidney stones. But it also had something to do with twilight itself, with its sense of life drawing back, retreating behind locked doors and shutters. With Ilona, the coming of darkness was an opening up, not a closing down. Life only begins at sundown, she told me once.

I reached up and pulled the chain on the lamp beside the phone, throwing the basement room into dim yellow light. Ilona had hung up on me. I thought: This is the way things end nowadays—with a telephone call. Voices on a wire tell you that life has changed, drastically, irreparably.

I reached up and pulled the lamp chain again. Real darkness filled the room. I stood up, felt for the car keys in my pocket, and headed toward the door.

"You don't give up, do you?" Ilona said when I appeared at the studio.

I stepped past her from the shadowy hallway into bright space. Almost immediately, I could tell that something was different about the studio. The broad expanse of floor, usually buried beneath canvases and paint cans, was bare. All of Ilona's paintings were stacked against the walls, and her brushes and supplies were pushed into a corner. The room looked like what it had once been—an empty warehouse. "I thought you were working tonight?" was the first thing that came out of my mouth.

"I came here to be alone, damn it. Damn you."

"I don't understand. . . ." I turned and saw a navy-blue dress hanging from the aluminum rack near the door. Beside it was a small green suitcase. "You're going," I said.

"To Knoxville. At 7:30 tomorrow morning. My Uncle Mike had a massive stroke." She stood with one hand on the open door.

I stared at her hand and couldn't think of anything to say.

"I got the message on my machine at home. I was going to call you from the airport and tell you. Then I would've been back after the funeral and that would've been it. We could've just picked up where we left off."

"You would've gone without seeing me?"

Ilona sighed, moving her hand down the door to the knob. "Look," she said, "give me a few hours, OK? Come back at eleven or something and we can spend the night here. But I need a few hours."

I felt totally disoriented, as if Ilona had been mouthing nonsense to me. But I understood the words. She was flying to a funeral in the morning, and she wanted me to leave. I stepped toward her and put my arms clumsily around her shoulders. "I'm sorry about Mike," I said.

"Me, too," Ilona said over my shoulder, crossing her arms tightly around my waist. We held each other for a few seconds; I expected at every moment to feel her sobs against my shoulder. Finally, she gently pushed my body away. "Come back at eleven."

I didn't move. "No," I said.

"What?"

"No, I'm not leaving."

Ilona crossed her arms in front of her. "I'm asking you to leave."

I walked past her, away from the door. "Ilona, no. I'm the guy you're seeing seriously, remember? You should need me here with you."

"I need a few hours alone, Roscoe." She uncrossed her arms, and then quickly crossed them again. "I can't believe you're doing this. I'm asking to be alone."

"Alone!" I shouted. I knew I was behaving terribly, but I couldn't stop myself. The resentment was welling up in me. "What the hell is wrong with you, anyway? Doesn't all this do anything to you?"

She stared at me with something like real hatred in her face. "You want drama, don't you," she said quietly, menacingly. "Convulsions, tears, the whole number. Like your little Armenian melodrama—sentimental moaning about people you've never even met. That's the way you want it, right?"

I kicked a chair—the only way my body seemed capable of responding. The chair skidded across the floor and fell over on its side.

"Get the hell out now," she said then, jerking the door wider. "Now!"

I looked at her face. The mouth was a straight, hard line. The nose seemed closer to bleeding than ever. "I'm going," I said. I walked past her again into the dim stairwell.

She slammed the door behind me, making the metal railings hum in their loose gray supports.

I went home first. I sat for an hour in my basement apartment, trying to do some reading for work, but the words on the page didn't make sense. Then I tried listening to music. I had the volume up so loud that Mr. Yamada came downstairs with a set of headphones, which he offered to lend me for as long as I needed them. He said that he also enjoyed listening to rock music at very high volume.

Finally, after watching my bedside clock flip all the minutes from 9:04 to 9:08, I got up, put on my shoes, and drove to the lab in Secaucus. Joyce was there, working late. "Just in time to help," she said, lifting up a cage full of white mice and carrying it across the room. The clock on the wall above her said 9:33. "Kraus is finished with all of these," she said, tossing her head toward the pile of cages in one corner of the lab. "A hundred and seventy-five mice to meet their maker this fine evening. And guess who got stuck with the dirty work."

Joyce put the cage down on a table. She reached her rubber-gloved hand into the cage and grabbed one of the mice by the tail. "Worst part of this damned job," she said as she spun it suddenly by the tail and cracked it hard against the marble tabletop. "Poor things." She tossed the dead mouse into a plastic garbage bag at her feet. "I could use a hand, if you've got a mind to," she said in a slightly louder voice.

"Sorry. I've got a ton of data to collate," I mumbled as I stepped toward my cubicle. No, I decided, I wouldn't tell Joyce. She would just shake her head knowingly, as if I were confirming something she already knew.

"Maybe next time," I heard as I shut the door of my cubicle. "Hell of a way to spend a Saturday night." Then: whiz, crack, thud, as another mouse tumbled into the slowly filling garbage bag.

When the phone beeped fifteen minutes later, I considered not answering. On the fifth beep, I grabbed it. "Listen, Roscoe," Ilona said without saying hello. "Come back at eleven, OK? We can spend the night out here."

I picked up a letter opener from my desk. "That's over an hour from now."

"At eleven," Ilona said.

From outside: whiz, crack, thud. Whiz, crack, thud.

"At eleven," I said finally into the plastic mouthpiece.

"It's 11:03," Ilona said as she pulled open the gray fire-door. "Did you hit traffic or something?"

"I was down in the parking lot. I guess my watch is slow."

Ilona pulled me into the room and closed the door behind me. "We'll have to leave here at six in the morning to get to Newark. I'll probably be gone for three days, so maybe you can water the aloes in the dining room on Monday. One pint of water for each." She led me across the room and sat me on the divan. "You can even stay there, if you want to. The house is full of groceries; they'll be rotting in three days anyway." She retrieved a bottle of vodka from the little refrigerator and brought it, with two shot glasses, over to the divan. It was obvious to me that we were to forget everything that had happened earlier in the evening. Ilona poured the vodka, handed me one of the glasses, and sat down beside me. "I'm going to hate the next three days," she said after a slight pause.

We drank the cold, metallic-tasting vodka in our glasses. Then I said: "I'm going."

Ilona's head snapped toward me, sending a bobby pin careening across the floor. "Where?"

"To Knoxville," I answered, staring into my shot glass.

Ilona put her hand on the inside of my thigh. "Roscoe," she began.

"I'm going to Knoxville with you, or else we're splitting up."

Ilona looked at me. Something seemed to change in her face, and then she took my glass and put it on the floor. "Well," she said at last, "let's hope Piedmont has an extra seat." She pulled my leg up over her own. "You want to try to sleep?" she asked.

"I won't be able to," I said. "Will you?"

"No. Not for a while, at least." She lay back on the divan, looking up at me until I stretched out beside her. "The lights are on," Ilona whispered.

"Let's leave them," I said. A large fly was in the studio. I could hear it across the room, buzzing and thudding against the walls.

"Try and sleep some," she said.

"I told you, I won't be able to."

"Well, just try, OK? I'll wake you up in plenty of time, don't worry. This time I even set the alarm." She shifted the weight of my head on her arm and put her other hand on the small of my back.

"You get some sleep, too," I said to her.

She pulled my body closer to hers. "It's a deal," she said.

6.

Ilona and I talk now about moving in together. The house in Englewood Cliffs, of course, could absorb me and my earthly possessions without even blinking. At idle moments during the day, I try to imagine my white Impala parked next to her white Lincoln in the semidetached garage, or my Flintstones jelly glasses standing next to her Danford Fire Department beer mugs in the kitchen cabinets. There's room for everything in that house.

It's been three weeks since we got back from the funeral. During our three days in Knoxville, not a single cloud appeared in the blue Tennessee sky. The trip almost seemed like a vacation. We even got to ride some of Mike's horses the day before we left, galloping along shaded country roads to a little pond, where we swam and ate cream-cheese-and-jelly sandwiches on a big rock crawling with salamanders.

The funeral itself was as unlike an Armenian funeral as I could imagine. Everyone looked marvelously fashionable in their dark suits and black mourning dresses. One woman—a cousin, I think—wore a wide-brimmed hat that kept flapping in the breeze. Later, during the funeral dinner at an Italian restaurant in Knoxville, people laughed and told funny anecdotes about Mike, as if it were a ceremonial dinner for someone who was retiring from the family firm. "Well, we got through it," Ilona said to me on the plane back to Newark. "Yes," I said, and I squeezed her hand, but I remember thinking, We got *through* it?

Since then, Ilona and I have become collaborators. At her suggestion, we're turning my article on Armenia into an "educational/aesthetic experience" with alternating pictures and text blocks. I'm rewriting the article—sticking to the pure facts this time—having sections of it printed on six-foot-square pieces of Plexiglas. Ilona is creating gigantic collages of maps, newspapers, and old photographs of victims of the massacre. She says she wants the show to inform the audience without imposing any kind of interpretation of the event. Bullshit, I say to myself, but I go along with it anyway. I enjoy working side by side with Ilona. Besides, the owner of Ilona's regular gallery in Paramus has agreed to sponsor the project and is trying to get funding for it from several private foundations and a group called the North Jersey Armenian-American Friendship Society (which even my parents have never heard of). The show is scheduled to open in December. My parents ("God willing," they say) are flying up for the opening-night cocktail party.

So this is our life now. The two of us spend enormous amounts of time together at the studio—me with my books and papers, Ilona with her glues and mud paints. We even sleep there occasionally. We've furnished the place with a double air mattress and a two-burner hotplate, so that we can disappear for days at a time—on cold, dreary weekends, leaving behind only an enigmatic message on Ilona's answering machine. On those weekends, I'll arrive after work on Friday with two orders from Fong's and a bottle of wine. We'll spend a few hours eating and drinking, then a few hours working. At eleven or midnight, we'll switch off all the lights, undress, and get under the covers on the limp air mattress. I'll turn to the all-news station on the radio next to the mattress. And then—amid the endless litany of fires, explosions, murders, and natural disasters—we'll gradually drift into sleep.

ABOUT THE AUTHOR

Gary Krist was born and raised in New Jersey. After graduating from Princeton, he began to write regularly for a variety of publications, including *The New York Times Book Review*, the *New Republic*, the *Hudson Review*, *National Geographic Traveler* and *Travel & Leisure*. He was awarded a grant from the National Endowment for the Arts, as well as the Sue Kaufman Prize for First Fiction from the American Academy and Institute of Arts and Letters, for *The Garden State*. He currently lives in Brooklyn with his wife and is at work on a novel.

VINTAGE
CONTEMPORARIES

V I N T A G E
CONTEMPORARIES

Now at your bookstore or call toll-free to order: 1·800·733·3000
(credit cards only).